SPECTRAL NOTES

Author Signatures

Cherie Baker
Colin Mitchell
Eric McFarlane
Evie Johnstone
George MacKinnon
Janet Crawford

Author Signatures

Jenifer Harley
Margaret Walker
Nadine Little
Robert Archibald
Stephen Shirres
Susi J. Smith

Spectral Notes

A collection of Halloween
Stories and Poetry
from
West Lothian Writers

Editors:
Cheryl Baker
Eric McFarlane
Janet Crawford
Stephen Shirres
Susi J. Smith

Published 2022
West Lothian Writers
www.westlothianwriters.org.uk

Print ISBN 978-1-4717-1909-7
Epub ISBN 978-1-4710-3978-2

Cover design and interior layout by Dragon Lime fantasy design : www.dragonlime.com

FORWARD

STEPHEN SHIRRES
West Lothian Writers Chair

At West Lothian Writers, we always celebrate Halloween in the same way, a writing challenge. Since 2013 we have asked our members to write a short piece (prose or poem) on the topic of Halloween to read out at the meeting closest to 31st October. Before Covid, the reading order was selected by choosing names from the Pumpkin of Doom, an orange bucket with a vaguely scary face. This tradition continues for our face-to-face meetings, but if it is a Zoom meeting, the chair picks a name at random, probably a more scary method, to be honest.

We get a huge range of pieces, whether it is old memories of guising in times past, horror stories of horrible things happening to horrible people or comedies about confused, old(er) women meeting traditional Halloween characters. This collection was created to bring these pieces together and celebrate them. However, many of the tales in this volume were written especially for it. It is up to you to guess which is which. We just ask you to enjoy them all equally.

AUTUMN'S SACRIFICE

NADINE LITTLE

Today, I am the chosen one.

The leaves outside are amber and gold and bronze. They blow and scrape across the concrete. I gaze in wonder. The air is crisp compared to the heated building we leave behind.

I don't look back.

The mother carries me to a car, her blonde hair tickling my face. Her two daughters dance around us, their blue eyes sparkling. The girls jiggle in their seats as we drive away, chattering like sparrows.

"I'm going to be scarier."

"Nuh-uh. I have sharp teeth and claws!"

"But I eat people."

"I drink their blood!"

A chorus of hissing fills the car. The mother—my mother, now—shakes her head, her lips curved in a smile.

Their house is a palace of glass and polished wood. We skip through on a grand tour, cinnamon spicing the air. Cobwebs dangle from the ceiling, witches caper on the walls. The girls show me their favourite toys: a stuffed bear missing an eye and a plastic dinosaur the colour of an aubergine.

"Come downstairs," the mother calls. "I need to get started if we're going to be ready for tonight."

Giggling, we rush into the kitchen, striped socks sliding on tile. I feel safe in their arms. Loved.

I sit on the marble counter shimmering with flecks of silver. My new family gathers around, their teeth flashing in wide grins. A bowl of chocolate eyeballs rests on the table.

I wish I could taste one.

The mother selects a serrated knife from a wooden block. The blade winks in the sunlight.

She stabs it into the top of my head.

The youngest girl claps her hands, leaning close, her sweet-scented breath caressing my skin.

"Careful. I don't want to cut you, too," my mother says.

I cannot run. I cannot scream.

The sawing motion rocks my body on the counter. The mother dispatches a slab of my head and brandishes a metal spoon. My innards splatter the marble. The older daughter swirls her fingernails through them and sucks on her hand. My flesh stains her chin.

I shriek inside my head, but the horror isn't done.

The knife slashes my face. Over and over and over. Chunks of tissue plop to the floor.

"Look at that mess," tsks the mother. "This is worse

than the last one. It wobbles too much."

I shiver and moan, but it makes no difference. She doesn't stop. They parade my butchered carcass through the house and place me on the porch for the entire world to see. No one bats an eye as I bleed into the grass, a rictus grin carved into my face.

Happy freaking Halloween.

WE NEED TO TALK ABOUT KEVIN'S IMAGINARY FRIEND

ROBERT ARCHIBALD

"Kevin!" The high-pitched shriek, equal parts rage and disbelief, broke the silence.

The vase lay in pieces. If it had been a 3-D puzzle, that might have been okay, however, as it was a family heirloom (very valuable, apparently, both in monetary and sentimental terms, as Kevin was often reminded!), then Kevin's mother was very unhappy.

Kevin, all four feet and two inches of him, stood over the debris, a large rubber ball in his hands. He turned round and looked up at his mother.

"It wasn't me," he said nervously.

"Really?" The one-word question managed to reach an octave higher than her original outburst. Kevin's mother looked around the room. "There are only the two of us here! Somehow I don't think it was the Invisible bloody Man! What have I told you about playing with balls in the house?"

"But... but... but..." Kevin stammered, his lower lip quivering. "It was Dick! He wanted to—"

"Stop right there." Kevin's mother held a hand up. "Your little imaginary friend didn't do this, did he?" She stared, defying Kevin to argue with her. "Put that ball away with your other toys," she continued, lowering her voice. "Go to your room. I don't want to hear a peep out of you. Is that clear?"

Kevin stared, anger flashing in his eyes. "You never believe me!" he cried. "Dick isn't pretend. He's real!"

"Just go to your room!" his mother cried in frustration. "I'll speak to your father about this later."

He stomped off, leaving his mother to sink to her knees and start picking up the tiny, broken pieces, tears welling in her eyes.

"We're going to have to do something, Jack," Kevin's mother said as they sat down at the dining table.

"Linda, he's a kid." Kevin's father sighed, throwing his jacket over the back of the chair. "We've talked about this." From his tone, that was as much as he wanted to say on the subject.

"That vase had been in my family for over a hundred years. You know how much it meant to me!" Kevin's mother snapped.

"Well, you should've taken it on Antiques Roadshow when you had the chance!" Kevin's father retorted.

"This isn't about money!"

"Look, he's just a kid. Of course, things are going to get broken. Didn't I tell you to put it away safe?"

"Christ's sake! Are you being deliberately obtuse? You know what I'm getting at. We need to talk about Kevin's imaginary friend. I'm really starting to worry about him. His teacher at school says he doesn't have any friends, he doesn't play with any of the other kids. Apparently, when they ask him, he tells them that he can't because Dick doesn't like him playing with anyone else!"

"It's just a phase—"

"You've been saying that for almost three bloody years now! It's not healthy! Look, maybe we need to think about, you know, getting him some kind of help—"

"What, like a bloody shrink?" Kevin's father barked out an incredulous laugh. "You think he's the first kid to have an imaginary friend? C'mon, get real!"

The argument would probably have continued for another while were it not for the sudden thumping noise which started above them.

"God, I swear, if he's playing with that bloody ball again, I'll--"

"Leave it, Linda," Kevin's father said, getting up. "I'll go up and speak to him, okay? I will make it clear that what he did was wrong and that he will be punished. Okay? And," he held up a hand to forestall any further comment, "I will speak to him about Dick, okay?" He smirked and winked.

"Oh, you're such a child!" Kevin's mother said, but she was fighting to keep a smile off her own face.

A gentle knock and the door was opened. Kevin's father peered into the bedroom and saw Kevin sitting on the floor, arms wrapped around himself, eyes red. There were no toys to be seen which puzzled the man, but he quickly dismissed this as it meant one less thing for him to worry about.

"Hiya, Kev," he said. "Mind if I come in?"

Kevin shrugged, refusing to look at his father.

"Your mum told me about what happened today."

"Wasn't my fault," Kevin mumbled.

"No, of course not, Kev. Accidents happen, right?" His father seemed pleased, probably thinking this was going to be easier than he had thought. "Thing is, sometimes even when we don't mean to do something, we still do it. That vase, well, it meant a lot to your mum. That's why she was angry when you... when it broke. Because it's old, it can't be fixed, do you understand? Like, um, when your granny Ada got, um, sick and, er, the doctors said, well, um, you know, what they said isn't really important right now. The point is—"

"But I didn't do it!" Kevin insisted.

"Now, Kev, what have we told you about telling lies?"

"It's the truth! It was Dick!"

"Dick," Kevin's father said softly. He let out a sigh. "Look, Kev, about Dick--"

"You see," Kevin continued, "we were playing tug. I was to grab onto Dick and pull as hard as I could and... and... Dad, why are you smiling?"

"What? No, I'm... it's... I mean..." Kevin's father bit down on his lower lip until he managed to compose himself. "Right, look, let's make a deal, you and me, okay?

8

Don't mention Dick to your mum--"

"But Dad, I want to play with him!" Kevin whined.

"Ssh, ssh, that's fine. You can play with him. Just don't tell your mum. Please?" Kevin gave a slow nod, a puzzled look on his face. "Oh, and before I forget, I told your mum I would punish you for breaking the vase. So, if she asks, I smacked your bottom. Okay?"

"Okay," Kevin answered.

"Good lad," Kevin's father said, standing up and ruffling the boy's hair.

The other boy shoved Kevin in the chest. "Ha-ha, you have a pretend friend! What a baby."

Kevin stepped back, mumbling, "No, no. I'll get into trouble. My mum—"

The boy leaned forward and raised his hands, ready to push again.

Nearby, the playground supervisor looked across in time to see Kevin's arms outstretched. The other boy, by this time, was lying on his back in a puddle of water.

"Kevin!" she called. "What have you done?"

She hurried over to help the other boy to his feet. Kneeling down, she looked him over. Tears lined his face and there were dark patches on his trousers and back but, otherwise he looked unhurt.

"Right, Kevin." she said, taking his hand. "It's the Headmaster's office for you."

Kevin's mother arrived at the school looking flustered. As she stormed along the corridor, she saw

Kevin sitting in a chair. The door to the office opened, allowing a woman to leave, leading a small boy away. She was short and round and waddled rather than walked, like a penguin. She glowered at Kevin, then spotted his mother.

"You need to control him!" penguin-woman snapped. "The boy obviously needs help, or maybe just a damn good thrashing."

Before Kevin's mother could respond, the woman and child hurried away. A man stood in the doorway. "Ah, you're here. Come in. You too, Kevin," he added.

Kevin and his mother entered the office and sat in the two chairs in front of a large desk. She dropped her handbag at her feet. The headmaster sat in the chair opposite them, hands steepled, a thoughtful expression on his face.

"We need to talk about Kevin," he began.

"Look, I'm sorry," Kevin's mother said. "I will make sure he apologises to the other boy. I'll get his clothes cleaned. It won't happen again."

"Unfortunately—"

"But it wasn't me!" Kevin wailed. "Why won't anyone believe me? It was Dick!"

"As you can see," the headmaster continued, "the problem goes beyond today's incident. I mean, what happened today is bad enough. This school has a zero-tolerance approach to bullying of any kind and--"

"Bullying? They're just boys! Obviously, I don't condone what Kevin did--"

"It wasn't me!"

"But the fact remains that, well, kids will be kids, yes?

Surely other children get involved in little spats!"

"That hardly justifies--"

"I'm not trying to justify anything!" Kevin's mother said through gritted teeth.

The headmaster looked at her, waiting until she had calmed down. "Kevin's imaginary friend, well, it's becoming... an issue. Naturally, at first no one was concerned, but after all this time... Kevin refuses to interact with other children. If they try to engage him, he tells them Dick doesn't want him to play. Any time he does something wrong, he always blames it on Dick." A sigh was followed by a cough as he cleared his throat. "Lately, some of the older children have been making all sorts of comments about Kevin 'playing with his Dick' and the younger children are asking what that means.

"You have to appreciate the school's position here. We have nearly two hundred pupils and, frankly, Kevin's behaviour is becoming more difficult to manage. We don't have the resources to give special care to a single pupil."

"What do you mean 'special'?"

"What I mean... What I'm trying to say is, I think you should have Kevin assessed. By a professional."

"My son is not crazy!" Kevin's mother said, her face turning red.

"No one said he is," the headmaster said quickly. "There are many medical conditions, such as ADHD, for instance, which can explain, er, unusual behaviour. If such a condition were diagnosed, obviously the school would be able to tailor the curriculum to meet Kevin's requirements." The headmaster paused, then said, "Please, discuss things with your husband. Then we can talk further."

The meeting over, Kevin followed his mother out to the car park. She gripped his wrist, almost pulling him along.

"Ow, Mummy!" Kevin yelped in pain.

"Oh, God, Kevin, I'm sorry," his mother said quickly, slowing her pace and releasing his arm. "I'm just... Oh, hell, I forgot my handbag." She stood Kevin beside her car and ordered him not to move. "I'll just be a moment," she shouted over her shoulder as she hurried back into the school.

Directly opposite was the space reserved for the headmaster's car.

Kevin's mother and father had had another loud argument that night, with no resolution having been reached. The next morning, they barely exchanged a word as they ate breakfast. While Kevin slurped more soggy Corn Flakes, there was a buzz and his mother picked her phone off the counter.

"My God!" she gasped.

"What's wrong?" Kevin's father asked.

"This text. It's from the... the school, the headmaster was involved in an accident last night. It seems his brakes failed and his car crashed into a tree. He's... he's dead."

"Oh, that's awful," Kevin's father said.

Kevin glanced away, as if staring into space. After a couple of seconds, he nodded and smiled.

After putting his plate in the sink, Kevin left the room.

"Guess that gives us some time," Kevin's father said.

"What?"

"Well, you know, if the headmaster's, um, you know,"

"Christ, Jack, a man has died!"

"I know, and it's terrible. But we've got to think about our son, haven't we?"

"By putting off a decision?"

"I just thought--"

"We can't put this off any longer. If there is something wrong with Kevin, the sooner we find out, the sooner we can do something about it."

Kevin's father looked pained. "Look, what if we transferred him to another sch--"

"How does that solve anything?" Kevin's mother demanded.

"I'm just throwing out suggestions!"

"Well, keep throwing, and I'll let you know when I hear a helpful one."

Both parents stayed quiet for a moment, the only sound the ticking of a clock.

"I'm... I'm sorry, Linda, okay? It's... it's just... I guess I don't want to think there's anything wrong with him. You understand?"

"Oh, of course I do." She took a breath. "Look, I'll phone around today, make some enquiries, see if I can get him an appointment."

He gave a resigned nod.

Kevin seemed to enjoy his day home from school, spending the time in his bedroom playing quietly. When his mother opened the door and said, "C'mon, Kevin. Your dad'll be home soon and we are going on a little trip."

"Is Daddy not working today?" Kevin asked.

"He was, but he's finished early so we can... go on a trip."

"Where are we going?"

"It's... it's a surprise." She smiled slightly before leaving. "Put your toys away and come and get your shoes and coat on."

Kevin's father opened the front door and looked up the stairs in front of him. At the top of the stairs stood Kevin's mother, Kevin right behind her.

A startled scream escaped her lips as she tumbled forward and down the stairs, landing with a sickening crack at the bottom.

As Kevin's father rushed forward, there was already a pool of blood spreading from Kevin's mother's head where it had struck the base of the banister. Horrified, he looked up the stairs where Kevin stood calmly.

"Kevin, what did you do?" The question came out as a whisper.

"Dick made me do it," Kevin replied. "He said, this way we can still be friends."

Kevin's father grabbed the telephone and dialled 999 as the tears formed in his eyes. As he waited for the paramedics to arrive, he sat beside the dead body, sobbing and mumbling.

"Why didn't I listen? Why didn't I listen?"

Kevin stood for a moment, staring down, before returning to his room to play.

"No!" Kevin screamed as the two men took his arms. "Not unless Dick can come, too."

One of the men glanced at the woman who was speaking with Kevin's father. She gave a slight nod, so the man told Kevin, "Sure, kid, whatever. The more the merrier, right?"

"We'll assess him tomorrow," the woman was saying.

"When can I come and see him?"

"Best to wait a couple of days. Let him get settled."

"Be a good lad, eh, Kev? You're just going on a little trip," Kevin's father said.

"A trip?" Kevin wiped tears from his face.

"Yes. You... and Dick. It'll be fun, like an adventure."

Kevin settled down and he was led to the back of a car, where he climbed in and sat between the two men. A short time later, he was led into a small, sparsely furnished room.

"This is where you'll be--" the doctor began.

"Wait! Where are you going?" Kevin cried, looking back along the corridor. "No, you said you'd stay with me!" This was followed by the sound of sobbing.

After that, well, I can't tell you about Kevin's fate. If the truth be told, he was a very good friend. In fact, in over two hundred years, he has probably been my best friend.

We were having so much fun together, and he was happy to do anything I told him to. It was perfect, and I didn't want it to end, so I tried to take care of any problems. Over the years, I have learned a lot from watching people, so I usually know what to do to get what I want.

Aren't I clever?

Except... except, I wasn't as clever as I thought, was I? All I did was help to bring about what I was trying to avoid; Kevin being taken away. By the time I realised my mistake, it was too late. I'm not strong enough to tackle more than one person at a time so I knew I couldn't keep Kevin at home so I told him I would go with him, just to keep him happy, but I couldn't stay in one of those places where everyone thinks there's something wrong with you. I had enough of them when I was alive.

I will just drift about for a little while. It shouldn't take me long to make a new friend.

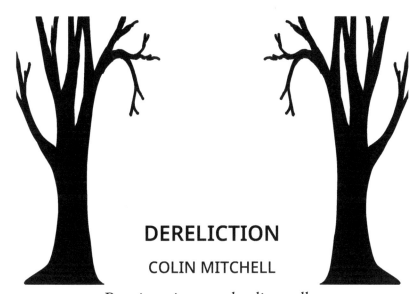

DERELICTION

COLIN MITCHELL

Rusting pipes on derelict walls,
Drips which echo in empty halls,
Flaking rotten window frame;
Things will never be the same;
Crumbling stone 'neath roofless gables,
Here neglect has turned the tables,
Turned this edifice once grand
To a blight upon the land.

Below the stone with crest and name
There's no oak door within its frame;
Coloured flagstones faded, cracked
Show the force of nature's act;

Oaken panels which lined the walls
Have vanished, gone to other halls;
Gaping fire like cavern door.
Mantel smashed across the floor.

Rotting timber letting nature
Give a home for living creature;
As in death, there is yet life
Midst this scene of morbid strife;
Where those elegant days of yore?
When ladies danced on ballroom floor
Servants proffered best champagne –
How I crave those days again.

Time was, I wandered through these rooms
Which now are chilled like empty tombs;
Windows framed with heavy drape –
Now like soul-less eyes they gape
Across a wilderness once known
As landscaped fields where trees had grown
Workers tending all that grew
In the gardens that I knew.

Imagination takes my mind
To hear and smell and see the kind
Of great joy once common here –

Sadness now invokes a tear;
These naked walls where creepers live
Have given all they have to give;
Ornate ceilings – all destroyed,
Nature has her might employed.
I hear the swish of silken gowns –
Rainbow colours, blacks and browns;
Men dressed in their finery,
Fruits of foreign winery;
Music dancing on harpsichord
Delights the ear of host and lord,
Powdered wigs and sparkling stones;
Whispered words in undertones.

Marble staircase to upper floors
Has gone the same way as the doors;
Rooms are now exposed to sky
As they too prepare to die;
The heart of this fine house is gone
And only I must linger on
In the place I met my death –
Where I breathed my final breath.

CREATURES OF
THE NIGHT

JENIFER HARLEY

'Twas the night before All Saints with the folks in town asleep.
She lay awake upon her bed, for it made her young flesh creep
to hear the lost and frightened scream; a haunting, eerie sound.
She rose and hurried to the scene; her duvet wrapped around.

"'Tis more than a soul can bear," she cried as she looked into the dark
and saw a flash of eyes, a screech, a swoop, then a lonesome bark.
Deep in the undergrowth, a being whimpered in the grass,
the evil pounce of a predator had swiftly come to pass.

'Til her dying day, she'll remember the happenings of that night
and she prayed to God that the shock had killed the thing with fright.
She watched helpless as a babe when claws sunk into the beast
then heard it ripped to pieces as the assassin got ready for the feast.

'Twill serve to remind such fools as dare go out on Halloween
that she'll have your guts for starters and then finish with your spleen.
And she doesn't care how fast you run, your sound she'll soon pick up
for after ripping out your heart the dripping blood she will then sup.

'Twasn't her fault that she witnessed this, she daren't resist a look
for she was forever changed that night with every breath she took.
A vulturous beast that stalks and strikes before the morning dew,
the end will come when you least expect; you'll bid the world adieu

'Tisn't it the plan of life that mother nature shows the way
and when she reached maturity, she was a wise old bird of prey.
Is she the hunter or the hunted – who'll survive – 'tis her or you?
And before she leaves her perch, she'll call T'wit – T'wit – T'woo

THE HAUNTING OF
BERNARD MCALISTER

ERIC MCFARLANE

It was a dark and stormy night when I went round Uncle Bernie's and I were soaked to the skinny when I got there. Course I'd put on my anorak and wellies but the anorak's got a hole at the shoulder and all the rain just went in and soaked my cardie which were really annoying 'cos it's my best cardie – the one with the purple stripes and the little glittery things what look like stars. I'm really fond of that cardie 'cos it was a special present from somebody or other who I just can't remember right now, but it will come to me. So I was thinking about my cardie being ruined, which is not a good thought and on top of that – well, not on top, but you know what I mean. On top of that, my wellies were leaking and my feet were sloshing about like two cod in a tank of cold water with bits of grit in it. So you can see that when I arrived at Uncle Berns, I was not a happy caravanner.

Uncle Bern's got this huge house on the edge of town. Don't know how he got to have one that size. Senga says he won the slaughtery which I think is her way of saying the lottery – you know the thing you buy tickets for from Jean in the Coop but when I said to her she tapped the side of her nose and said, I know what I mean, luv. She's deep is Senga. I've always said that. Actual fact I don't think Bern's a real uncle, know what I mean? We had ever so many uncles when I were little and I think some of them were imaginary uncles like uncle Sergei who was a sailor.

So, as you may imagine, I was not in my sunny-day mood when I knocked at the big knocker on Bernie's door. No one answered. I knocked harder but that stupid knocker was rusty and it broke off just like one of those long French baggots you get at Tesco half price if you go in late evening.

I was left there, standing like a tube of Smarties, soaked through, holding my knocker and no answer. Then there was a sudden noise, the door flew open, and this woman sprinted out like Jenner's sale had just opened. Skinny woman, older than me with a weird hair-cut, but she was gone so quick I couldn't get a proper look. Sounded like she was shouting run. Maybe the housekeeper.

Well, I marched right in. I'd had enough of standing in the rain and shrinking. Did you know that damp affects the brain? It was on Channel 4 a few weeks ago. You see, you think that your skull is all hard like a helmet, but actually it's full of holes like a cheese grater- not big holes, really tiny holes like parmesan. Then the water can seep into the holes, and it can affect your mind. That's why we're sad when it rains because our brain's all soggy and heavy and then the sun comes out and we're happy, as long as it's not out too long.

"Bernie," I shouted, standing in the hall. "You there?" The words sort of echoed around and came right back to me.

The hallway was huge, all dark wood with a wide staircase in front and on the right a grandfather clock going ticky-tocky. And then the front door shut behind me with a bang that would have dropped your drawers. I could hardly see nothing, just the shadow of the stairway and some gloomy old pictures up on the walls.

"Bernie, you playing your games again?" I shouted. He was always a right one for the games was Bernie. Mam and I played hide and seek with him one Christmas. I won. I waited absolutely ages in the coal bin around the back door and they never found me. So I went back in and there's the two of them having a wee sherry at the kitchen table. "You win, pet," Bernie shouts at me when I came in the door. "Best damn hider in the business you are."

Mam just sat there. Her face was all red, and she was out of breath, like she'd been running. They must have looked everywhere, so I were real pleased with myself.

"I'm not playing," I shouted up the stairs, but there was no answer. I walked to the foot of the steps. "You can just come out right now, Bernard McAllister. I'm fed up with your nonsense." It wasn't like me. I'm usually politer but as I may have said already, I was not pleased.

Then it seemed to get brighter and this great shadow reared up in front of me. I knew it was only my shadow, of course, but it gave me a bit of a frightener, as I'm sure it would you and all. When I turned about, I saw a great white light shining through the window. The rain had gone off, and the moon had come out and it was a full one too, really bright and shining. It's amazing to think that men have walked on the moon way up there. At least I think they were all men. Perhaps they don't allow women on the moon for some reason. I suppose if you had men and women together in these little module things, it wouldn't be right. They'd be rubbing against each other every time they turned around and what with one thing and another and those uncontrollable urges that men have, you know, to go where no man has gone before, even if perhaps they have gone before, there's no knowing what might happen in the circumstances and it might lead to embarrassments or even an edition of Big Brother from space which would make eviction interesting don't you think? Anyway, it was when the moon came out that I heard it. A howl.

A long, creepy howl that would have scared the what nots of a thingummy. Didn't bother me 'cos I knew it was only a dog. Perhaps someone had stood on its tail. Only funny thing was it seemed to be coming from upstairs. Another thing – I knew Bernie didn't have a dog. At least he didn't last time I saw him. Said he was allergic to them like with peanuts. Of course, that might have changed. They can cure peanuts, I heard, perhaps they can cure dogs. Now, I'm not a dog lover. Never had one as a pet. When I were little, we had a budgie, what we called Budgie, and then a spider monkey, what we called Spidy, and then a gecko, what we called Albert. You see, Mam had started her taxidermy class by then, so we went through a lot of pets. She kept saying the only way to get better is to practise, which is true of course. So I was glad we never had a dog. But as I say, dogs don't bother me none. So when I saw this great hound come trotting down the stairs large as life and just as ugly it never worried me neither.

It had a pointed head and great big snarly teeth that it was showing off. There were great dribbles of drool drooling down its jaw and landing on the floor, splat, splat. Someone was going to have a mess to clear up, that was for sure.

"Hello, boy," I said and put my hand out to pat the creature. Well, the ungrateful brute tried to bite me so I slapped it on the muzzle with my handbag. In my experience you have to show a dog who's boss. Same with children. If they misbehave, a good wallop with the handbag will sort it. I suppose you can't do that there now with children but you can with dogs. And it worked. It moaned and sat there on the step giving me big soulful eyes and drools.

"There, there boy," I said. "Take me to your master. There's a good doggy."

Well, it reared up on its hind legs and gave a great howl again before bounding up them stairs like nobody's business. It had disappeared before I even started up, but

I just followed the big splats of drool on the carpet. I followed it right to the top of the house, which is three floors, so I was fair wore out when I got to the top. Senga says I'm not fit, but she's a fine one to talk. Miss just-one-more-won't-do-me-any-harm. I was stood outside a door. I could hear the dog inside, rushing about hither and yonder like it was posessioned. Up above me were three skylights what let some light in but it was really dark. Now I'm not scared of the dark, but it's not generally the dark that does you any harm. It's what you don't see that does it, like tripping over a dead salmon for instance.

"Bernie, you in there?" I knocked on the bedroom door and all of a sudden the scurrying stopped and at the same time it got really dark and I could see up above that the moon had gone away. "Bernie. You let me in this minute, you hear," I yelled. Then the door creaked open and all I could see was this black space. There was a horrible smell too and the sound of heavy breathing like our coalman used to do after he'd dropped one in the bunker or our fishman after Mam had paid him in kind. How can you pay a fishman in kind? I mean... well, how?

Anyway, thank Polly Pumpkin that the light came on then. And there's Bernie standing at the door with his hand on the switch and looking a sight. His clothes was all shredded to bits, his hair were too long, and it was him that was doing the panting.

"Where's that dog of yours?" I asked him.

"Seline. What you doing here?"

I could hardly make him out. His voice was all growly and his eyes were bloodshot and horrible. "Bernard Mc-

Allister, you have been drinking again. What did the doctor tell you?"

"Hah, won't be tellin' me nothin' no more, that's for sure. God's sake. Why're you here?"

"That's a fine question," I said. And you know what? I couldn't remember why I were there. It had gone completely.

His eyes slithered around in his head. "You should go. Moon might be out soon."

"It's a full one. We could watch it together."

"No, no, no. You need to go. Go now. It takes over. I'm not responsible." He grabbed me with his big hairy hand and practically threw me downstairs.

Well, I wasn't having none of that. I'm a quiet sort. I keep myself to myself in spite of what Senga may say. But he'd gone too far.

"Bernard McAllister. You'll not get away with throwing me away like some coal sack that's empty of coal and is no use for anything except more coal. I've a good mind to do something... or other. So just you watch out."

I listened but there wasn't a sound, just some shuffling around. Then the dog started up again, howling, howling like it was starving. So much noise.

"Right," I shouted. "I've had enough. I'm going home. If you don't look after that dog better, I'll report you to the dog people what look after dogs."

I turned around and headed downstairs. That big drooly thing was following me. I could hear its pants going pant, pant and its paws going pad, pad on the stairs. My legs started going a wee bit faster, and I shouted back,

"You need to get a poodle or a shits you."

That dog sounded like it was getting bigger and louder. When I reached the front door I was running. I yanked the door open and nearly collided with a woman standing there. Older than me with a weird haircut, but I wasn't going to stand there and talk about hairdressing. "Run," I yelled and raced off down the driveway.

But I wasn't long home when I got to thinking – I'd left Bernie alone with that big dog. Did he know how to control it? And that woman, she might need help. So I had a cuppa and set off back to Bernie's.

It was a dark and stormy night when...

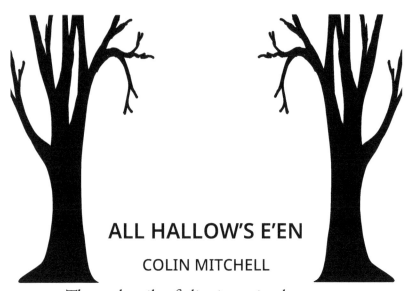

ALL HALLOW'S E'EN

COLIN MITCHELL

Through veils of clinging mist they come
To seek out living souls
An odour wafts – too much for some
Who scurry back to holes
Where they feel safe from evil fiends
Which roam the earth tonight
From eerie marble figurines
To woodland pest, the sprite

This very night the underworld
Breaks forth this land to rule
The frightened stay indoors, all curled
Away from creatures cruel
But ghosts and spectres can't be held
At bay as through the walls

To find the living they're propelled
With wailing, piercing calls

And yet, a non-believer walks
A sodden, lonely path
Not knowing what it is that stalks
Or even yet the wrath
Which, silent, grows inside this beast
Until it finds the chance
On this fresh specimen to feast
Without a second glance

No sound he hears as ever near
Death slithers by his side
Too late! And now no time to fear
He sees, eyes opened wide
The foul red-eyed demon bites
Jaws dripping, closing fast
As scarlet on torn clothes alights
The poor fool breathes his last.

THE HALLOWEEN CHICK

CHERIE BAKER

The Halloween chick's got a list, but she doesn't need to check it twice. It's all naughty. I dropped to my belly, and Herself hopped off my shoulder. The shadow of the steps were dark. Hopefully dark enough to hide even a misfit like me.

Downy yellow fluff on stick-like legs ambled up to the suburban condo's door. She cheeped. Traffic drowned out the small noise. Light flickered through the curtains, but no one answered the door. A long tentacle sprouted from the chicks head. It pressed the doorbell.

"Will you get that, Hon." A woman's voice echoed through the thin walls.

"It's midnight... Probably pranksters," a man answered.

The chick rang the bell again. A few minutes later, a woman in flannel pyjamas opened the door.

She looked up and down the deserted street. "Fucking Halloween jokers..." she mumbled and turned.

The chick peeped and hopped up to the woman's bare toes.

The woman crouched down. "Little shite bags left you? Not much of a prank, you're too cute." She reached out.

A flurry of fluff and feathers revealed the demon's true face. The woman collapsed.

H.C. clucked a satisfied chirp and sprinted away, vaulting onto my back. "Tally ho pumpkin."

I sprang up. Galloping to reach escape velocity, then leaped. The ground dropped away, and we sailed over rooftops.

I've no idea why they call me pumpkin. I'm not even remotely pumpkin shaped or coloured. Maybe ginger at a push, but I like to consider myself golden... Not that that fits a hell-hound either. I bit back a sigh. At least they let me have a real assignment this Halloween. Not like the usual drivel given to a misfit like me.

H.C. tapped her list. "So many this year. We may not get to all of them."

A low growl rumbled in my throat. She knew the rules. Just because my colours don't match the rest of the pack didn't mean I was stupid. "You get one hour Demon. No more."

She snorted. "Shame. The last one has a greenhouse full of flowers."

My heart clenched. I'd never smelled a flower. "How many more?"

"Fifty four."

Normally I did not care what my charges did on their yearly parole, but the chance to smell a real flower was too good to miss. I did the sums. One death a minute would be tight but possible.

"Hold on and do not dally with your fun." My speed increased until I was running as fast as magic allowed.

H.C. popped on and off my back like a turbo-charged Yo-Yo. Bodies frozen in terror fell as thick as the autumnal leaves, but the witching hour was closing just as quickly. Hell's barren sandy expanse overlapped the dark dampness of earth.

"It's time." I said and turned toward home. Disappointment squeezed my gut. Flaming monkey skulls, sniffing flowers would have to wait until next year.

The chick pulled the soft hair around my ears. "Stop, this is it." She pointed to an old Victorian building with a large glasshouse on the south side. Green foliage dotted pressed against the glazing. "This won't take long, and it's only one minute past midnight..."

Her pleas matched my own desire, but was there really enough time? I'd never hear the end of it if I lost a class one demon. My colouring was enough of a laughing-stock already, I didn't need the extra grief.

"I love Jasmine, it's just heavenly you know... Oh, how silly of me. Pumpkin, the deformed hell-hound, doesn't get out much. Of course, you don't know what flowers smell like." The demon laughed and slapped my neck.

Fuck it. I wasn't going to be made fun of by an imp.

I sprang back to earth. The edges of the portal brushed my shoulders. It was shrinking by the second. I landed and crashed through the glazing of the greenhouse.

A light flipped on in the house. A frail man looked out a window.

H.C. hopped off while I galloped through the greenery sniffing. All greenery... Rows and rows of ferns and palms. No flowers. Bloody demon had lied. What a surprise.

The demon jumped up to a window ledge. I swiped her off with a paw and snatched for the punk, but the pipsqueak ran for the front door. Stupid demon—deception and avoidance would only add to her punishments once we got back.

I galloped after the ball of fluff and grabbed her in my teeth. The front door opened and a thin man with white hair stepped out. He threw a ceramic pot. His aim was good. It hit the back of my head, knocking the demon out of my jaws and me into the doorway home.

The portal to hell closed in around me, reducing my vision of earth to a pinpoint. The man cradled the chick in one hand and flipped a rude gesture at me with the other.

Laughter erupted from the other hell-hounds. "Pumpkin, pumpkin, roly-poly bumpkin."

The lady of our land waved her hand. "Leave Pumpkin be and take up your posts. The demon played an unfair game. We shall have a fine hunt for it next year."

My siblings trotted to their stony perches to guard the gates.

What was done, was done. It could not be undone until next year. I sighed and shook my whole body, throwing away the worry and angst. Dirt and blue porcelain slid off my shoulders, followed by a leafy red geranium. I buried my nose in it and heaved in a heavenly scent that blotted out the stench of sulphur. It was magnificent.

I picked the plant up with my teeth and returned to my spot in front of the Goddess' throne. A year wouldn't be so long to wait with my new perfume.

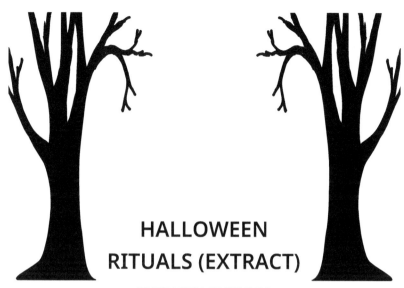

HALLOWEEN RITUALS (EXTRACT)

STEPHEN SHIRRES

For as long as we've known each other, Lucy and I do the same thing every Halloween. We watch scary movies. Not the usual ones that appear on the best of lists. We look for the fun ones, the stupid over the top ones. Any era from any place, we don't care whether they are black and white or colour, silent or sound or from what part of the global they hail from.

Ideally, we want them on the biggest screen possible, surrounded by a crowd of strangers screaming and laughing along with the silliness. We have yet to manage an IMAX screening. They are too self-important for our kind of movies. The Indy cinemas are normally where we end up. If only there was a Prince Charles in every town and city across the country. Their all-night movie marathons are the ideal for what we want. Londoners don't know how lucky they are.

Occasionally, one of the mainstream cinemas shows our kinds of film but only if it is a new release or some kind of anniversary. Tonight we got lucky with a double bill of horror stupidity at the Premier Film Cinemas on the edge of town.

The out of town retail park is more industrial estate now. The once colourful sign, promised shops and fun, has been replaced black and white grid of a map. Only the cinema has survived the takeover.

"Don't say it." Lucy parked right outside the front door. Behind us is a desert of concrete interrupted by a smattering of parked cars, an oasis of colour in the grey.

"Say what?" I looked across at her, confused.

"The rant, cinemas should be modern day cathedrals to the gods of the silver screen etc and so on." Her hands spoke the words with her. Her expression is one of mock boredom, or at least that is what I hope it is.

"I hardly think some grand art déco or Gothic cinema was destroyed to build this shed of a building." I opened the car door and got out. "Chances are the only things that lost out when they opened this place were the animals in the fields they built on."

The neon sign bathed us in the pink lights of dusk. More cinemas need bright, louder signage. Giant four floor movie posters have their place but they disappeared into the building after a while. Neon just screams for attention.

The vast entrance hall of the cinema demanded silence, however. Only the popping popcorn rebelled against the oppressive requirement. Like the grand cathedrals which force you into whispered conversations. I smile. Lucy knows me too well. Old memories stir, hot butter mixing with the sizzling meat of the hot dogs rolling over and over and over again. Ticket halls filled with people all talking rhubarb to each other.

A door clicked, the memory gone. At the furthest concession stand, a figure appeared. We walked towards them, keeping our footsteps as quiet as we can. A teenage boy, all spots and curly hair, limbs loose as if he can't be bothered to hold them up, greeted us with the same dull energy. "Hello."

"Two tickets for the Halloween double bill, please?"

"She-Dracula & the Harlot Nuns and Orgy of the Dead?"

I look at Lucy. "You didn't tell me that was what they were called."

"What?"

"They sound like soft-core porn films. T&A flicks from knock off movie studios."

"All our favourite films are bad 1960s horrors from Poverty Row studios."

The teenager watched us argue as if the result doesn't affect him either way. Probably not on commission then.

"Ed Wood wrote the second one."

I sighed with defeat. She knows I'll never turn down an Ed Wood film. There is something about his ambitious ideas being realised on a budget of £4.50 that I love. I turn to the teenager. "Two for She-Dracula & the Harlot Nuns and Orgy of the Dead."

"Don't forget the popcorn." Lucy adds. "A very large

one, please."

"Make that two." These films are the very definition of popcorn movies.

Suitably, the films were being shown in screen 13. It must be the smallest room Premier Film Cinemas has, fifty seats max squared off in seven rows. The screen itself looked smaller than my Mum and Dad's giant TV they have a home, their latest skiing trip or, as I call it, spending my inheritance. The door gave a Halloween style creak as we entered. We have been given numbered seats, but they'd been taken by three teenage girls, the only other people in the cinema, so we claimed the back row – as far as away from the interlopers as we could manage. Neither of us believe in talking during a movie unless we have the cinema to ourselves or the film was really, really, really terrible. Both these films were likely to fall into the latter category.

The lights darkened and the cinema's standard welcome messages started, suggesting we buy popcorn and drinks. Lucy held up each item to the screen as they were mentioned. Moments after we were told to leave by the fire exits once the film was finished, so we could get to the car park faster, the house lights went back up again. Standing to the left-hand side of the screen was a tall, thin, androgynous man, in a top hat and very long black cloak, which covered his shoes.

"Welcome," he began in a voice as deep as Christopher Lee's. "To our Halloween spectacular double bill. Please enjoy tonight's frights."

"Who was that?" I whisper.

"The manager," Lucy replied. "Kind of a character, according to Mina."

"In a good or a bad way."

"Both unfortunately. Mina learnt the hard way never to be left alone with him. A bit touchy." She put air quotes around the last word. I don't want to know more. Tonight was about fun horror, not the real life kind.

"But now." Our host recaptured our attention. "Time for the ultimate combination of 1960s sex and horror. Vampires and supple young virgins of the female variety." He flashed a smile, which confirmed everything Mina had said about him. "Please be encapsulated, hypnotised even, by tonight's star attraction, She-Dracula & the Harlot Nuns."

The lights dimmed to black. The screen lit up. More laughter, this time from the sound system, announced the film's studio logo, an animated man biting into the neck of a clearly naked woman. My concerns at the ticket desk returned. This was going to be soft-core porn dressed in horror iconography, less scary than the Scooby Doo Halloween Special. I slid down into my seat with a silent groan. At least these films are normally short.

The titles gave way to a dorm room. Rows of beds down each side. A group of three blonde haired teenage girls, clearly novices, played by actresses ten years old than their characters, sat huddled around each other on one of the bed. They all wore the same basically see-through white night dress. I could hear Lucy's after film commentary on the sexualisation of girls barely of legal age. At

41

least it was something to look forward to.

"What happened to Lucy?" One novice said to the others in hushed tones.

"She's called Lucy." I whispered.

'I know,' Lucy mouthed and pointed me back to the screen just as another character said, "All they'll say is she left." None of them have revealed their character names so far, despite them all looking the same in a village of the damned kind of way.

"She was walking by the vampire's castle, is what I heard." The second one's face suggests the location should scare us. I'm surprised the soundtrack didn't reinforce the idea or the film maker added a crack of lightning. Almost suitable for films of this vintage.

"I heard she was doing more than walking. With a statue of the Virgin Mary as well."

My laughter filled the screening. One of the teenagers in front of us hushed me. Lucy scolded me instead. "You didn't laugh when they showed it actually happening in Benedetta."

"That is a matter of historical record. This..." I pointed at the screen. "is pure nonsense."

"It's only just started. Like less than five minutes in."

Again, we are hushed by the same teenager. At least they've been brought up correctly.

"Maybe she got lost." The first on-screen novice asked. She is clearly the innocent of the group. Her two friends gave each other a look that of all Film-Lucy's possible fates, being lost isn't one of them.

Knock! Knock! Knock!

Loud and crashing. Sound system blared out the most unsubtle music cues I've ever heard. Stringed instruments screaming their loudest cries of 'this-is-scary.' The second novice is unfazed. The Practical Novice, until the film gives her an actual name, walked towards a window. How she knows which one was knocked on, I don't know. The film certainly doesn't give any clue. It is more concern with how her body moved under the nightgown. At her rain splashed chosen window, she reached up for the latch, a hook of black metal.

Knock! Knock! Knock!

The knock returned with the same thuddingly obvious music cue. The Practical Novice screamed. Her companions ran to her side and huddle together, all looking up. Cartoonish expressions of horror plastered across their faces as if the audience doesn't understand what is happening.

"What is it?" One of them asked. I can't tell which one. The camera is far more interested in the window. There is nothing there beyond the splash, splash, splash of rain on glass. I'm guessing it is the Naïve Novice. The one who thought Film-Lucy got lost in the woods. I haven't thought of a nickname for the third one yet.

The Naïve Novice made the suggestion they only make in bad horror movies. "We should let them in. As Mother Superior says, Our Lady Immaculate turns no one away."

"If they have enough money." The third one added, christening herself, the Cynical Novice. It'll do until another nickname suggests itself.

"Only one way to find out." The Practical Novice joked, a defence mechanism as clear as day. Again, she reached up for the window latch. The film slowed down. The cinematic countdown before another knock. Quiet, quiet, bang as one film critic once described it. Her finger touched the metal. Still no noise, the soundtrack is silent. The hook stiff in the hole, the way a latch should be in a horror movie. Got to build up the tension. The knock will come at any moment.

With a dink, the latch popped out; the hooks swung free. Both windows flew open and the music cue roared to the darkness revealed. The rain sparkled the novice's nightdresses. The music dropped again, almost silent now, another countdown to reveal who had knocked. Each note, a footstep. They started as a shape, undefined by name, then a shadow, human by outline. The camera cut to her long damp hair, darkened by the rain, plastered to her see-through nightdress. The same design as the novices. She has the same floating walk as the cinema owner, the hem unmoved. This must be Lucy, our lost wanderer in the woods. At the threshold of the window, she stopped, her arms out wide, her whole body on display.

"By opening this window, you welcome me in. You heard my request and answered it." Her face now filled the screen. Her eyes go blood red, her irises black to match her pupils. "Look into my eyes." Black and red spun in opposite directions, the colours rotated over and over. The effect was bloody impressive for the 1960s. The film is too old for CGI and the human eye just doesn't move like that. They seemed to swell, taking over her face until the whole screen was red with two black circles merging into one. All the time she kept repeating, "Look into my eyes. Look into my eyes and become my servants. Become the servants of She-Dracula."

I chuckled. No one else did.

"We are the servants of She-Dracula." The three novices said, their eyes the same red colour as the woman who commanded them.

"We are the servants of She-Dracula." The four women in the audience repeated. I looked across at Lucy with the same transfixed stare as the characters on the screen. I nudged her but got no response. She sat unmoved, staring straight ahead, repeating the now ominous line over and over in a monotonous tone.

"We are the servants of She-Dracula."

I nudged her again, harder, but no response. The film was doing something to her. I had to break her concentration. Only one thing to do. I reached across and covered her eyes.

"What are you doing?" Lucy sounded herself again. Her hand pulled at my mine.

"Not till you turn away from the screen."

"What? Are you mad?"

"Please." The ridiculousness of the situation dawned. The three teenagers must be under the same spell as Lucy had been, otherwise they'd have told me off by now.

"Fine." She turned her head. I let my hand fall away as she did so. "What the bloody heck was that all about?"

"The film did something to you."

She had never looked at me so witheringly before. "You sound like a Daily Mail column. Film don't do things to people. There have been –"

"We are the servants of She-Dracula." The teenagers and the novices say together.

Lucy turned back to the screen.

LIZZIE

EVIE JOHNSTONE

The kitchen clock read 'five to' and she had said half past.

"I am a volunteer," she chided herself, grabbing her flask and her heavy duty gardening gloves. "Still, I should be there when I said I would."

Meg grabbed her 'toolkit'. It was a canvas supermarket bag, stuffed with an old sheet, her trowel, secateurs, a kneeling pad (God – don't forget that). Shoving the flask and her gloves on the top she patted her pocket. "Keys, car keys?" and was out the door, running to her car.

She checked the time as she turned in at the church gates. It was just after quarter past. She drove round to the little car park. Unless there was a funeral no-one used it on Thursday mornings. Thankfully, for Meg didn't like manoeuvring her car. Truth be told she was never very good at it!

Tool bag slung on her shoulder, she pointed the key

fob at her little Fiat. The lights flashed as though waving her off and she walked over to the cemetery wall. This was her third visit. Meg was one of life's volunteers. She had been doing the flowers in the church every fourth Saturday for about a year when Reverend Robertson collared her a few weeks back. She was admiring her arrangement of spring flowers in the baptism font. "Meg" he'd said, and she jumped. There he was with his wee smiley face. "So glad I've caught you today."

"Oh aye Rev?" The minister was a round, little man. Fond of a scone and three sugars in his tea. She drew herself up so that he had to crane his neck but it didn't deter him.

"You do such a lovely job with the flowers Meg. I've been wondering. . ." He put his head on one side and then added. "The graveyard is looking so overgrown."

'If he thinks I'm going to volunteer to cut the grass, he is sadly mistaken!'.

Her face must have betrayed her thoughts because he rushed on. "It's the graves Meg. Some of them are" – he made air quotes with his fingers - "so unloved."

So here she was – on her third Thursday – the "carer of the unloved". She mimicked the finger movements. That first time she had gone round, cemetery plan in hand, figuring out the alphabetical layout and the number plaques on headstones. She had met and consulted with George, the part time grave digger, and had finally persuaded herself that she should tidy one of the graves – just to see how it felt. Walking among dead people

48

seemed plain weird to Meg!

Much to her surprise, it turned out to be very different to what she had expected.

By nature Meg was a tidy person. The leaves and the weeds needed lifting. Flower vases should be straight. The yew trees - much beloved by cemeteries - were collaborating with the ivy to hide several of the graves and moss was obscuring the names.

It wasn't long before Meg was engrossed in her task. Trimming, clipping, endless trips with her bag of weeds to the big bins at the gate. She even found herself chatting to the 'occupants'. Once she uncovered the inscriptions and the names, they were people to her. "There you go Mr Fraser. Ye'll get a bit o' the sun now!" At one point she had laughed out loud as she crossed between two stones, patting them both as she went and apologising for stepping through.

Still smiling at the memory, Meg unfolded her plan, opened the gate and walked out onto the short, mossy grass. George was whistling away on the far side and she raised her hand to him as she strode along. I want row J. In front of her was N. To its left was M so she was going left. "Aha! There's K'"

A voice close by said "This is row J, this one here."

Meg automatically answered, "Thank you," but she glanced up, puzzled, to see a little girl standing on the path. She looked about seven or eight, pigtails, such a pretty face.

The child skipped over. "Are you making it all tidy again?"

Meg looked around. "Well I'm trying."

"My grandad thinks you're doing a great job." She turned and pointed to an older gentleman sitting on a bench three rows over.

Meg set her bag down and stretched out her hand. "My name is Meg. Pleased to meet you." She put a question in her voice.

"I'm Lizzie." The little girl didn't offer a hand in return but danced off across the grass to her grandfather. He waved to Meg and she could see them put their heads together.

She walked to the bottom of row J, laid her bag down, chucked the kneeling mat in front of the first stone and began her tidying. "Strange the wee one wasn't at school today. Was that a school uniform? Little beret on her head, blazer, one sock further down than the other. Probably a fancy girl's school somewhere."

Time moved on and, satisfied with her work, Meg was examining the next untidy lair when Lizzie appeared at her side, pointing at the number plaque. "This is No. 10. Will you get to 18 today?"

"Em, I might if the ones in between aren't too untidy."

Lizzie hopped from foot to foot. Her grandfather called her, but she flapped a hand at him. "Will you see if you can make it today?" she wheedled.

Meg smiled. "C'mon then. Let's look." Getting up was a chore, but she managed it with the help of somebody called Annie Calder. She brushed her knees and joined the child.

She was about to ask why No. 18 was important when Lizzie started pointing. "14's not bad, and look, 16's tidy."

Next was an overgrown yew whose branches were tangled with bramble. Tendrils of ivy fighting for light.

Meg's heart was sinking as she stared at the mess. "No. 18?"

Lizzie nodded sadly. She looked back down the row with such a wistful expression Meg sighed. "Okay you win. No. 18 is next." She went off to empty her weed bag and collect her belongings.

"Cup of tea, I think, before I start on this one." Lifting the flask, she strolled over to the bench. The man made space for her to sit. She held out one of the cups. "Would you like some tea? There's plenty."

He had a lovely smile, sad around the eyes though. "No thanks, we're fine lass." Lizzie sat between them, legs swinging. He gestured at the rows of graves. "You've got some job here."

"Oh, tell me about it! I like it though and I'm just a volunteer." She poured her tea and sat back, enjoying the peace. After a few minutes Lizzie slid off the bench and walked away towards the church.

Meg watched her go saying, "She's lovely. Knows her own mind I think."

"That she does. Keeps me right! My son's daughter."

"Well it's very nice to meet you both Mr..."

"Loveboyd, m'dear. Harry Loveboyd."

Tea gone, Meg wandered back over to view No 18.

She spread her old sheet at the front of the tangle. That made it easier to move the clippings to the bin. Gloves on, she carefully parted the foliage and there, completely hidden, stood a stone. When she pushed a bit further in she could make out the date, 1959.

Before long several branches of the old yew were in the bins, she was lacerated by the brambles but, at least you could see the stone.

Lizzie came to inspect her work. She watched as Meg pulled endless strands of ivy that would drag more brambles to thwack her face and arms.

It was strange though. Part of her would have given up for another day but she had such a sense that someone wanted to be found. She stretched. "Right then." The child grabbed the beret from her head, threw it in the air, then she plonked it back, tossed her pigtails and ran off to her granddad again. They both waved to her, and she waved back.

"Who are you?" she said to the stone.

It took another hour before the ground was clear and the weeds were out of the way. It had a lot of moss on its face and Meg was peering at it when Lizzie came towards her. She stared at Meg for several seconds, lifted her hand in a shy little wave. Then she blew Meg a kiss, turned and walked away.

"How sweet, did her grandfather send her over? What did he say his name was? Loveboyd? Yes that was it."

She knelt closer to the headstone, using her index finger to move the lichens and trace the letters.

"In memory of." Right, got that! She leaned back a little. "Where's the date gone?" She found it. 1959 — 22nd May, 1959. "Oh isn't that funny? Today's the 22nd of May." Some of the bits of moss fell off in her hand. Elizabeth... and underneath accident. Then loving something. More moss came away, and she read Harry.

She gripped the top of the stone and, as gently as she could, rubbed at the letters with her forefinger and thumb. Her hand shook as the last of the moss came away.

In Memory

of

Elizabeth Loveboyd aged 8

and

her loving granddad

Harry Loveboyd

taken in a tragic road accident

22 May 1959

Meg stared at the simple words and then scrambled to her feet. She knew, in her heart of hearts, what she would see – and she smiled.

The bench was empty.

CAREFUL WHAT
YOU WISH FOR

JENIFER HARLEY

The scent of candle wax hung over the room and oily air stung Sarah's eyes. The handmaiden's stitching was the envy of all seamstresses in the village but tonight she knew, even with all her skills, it would be impossible to finish the gown. A blister on her finger burst and yellow puss dripped downwards. The dress crumpled at her feet as she covered the seeping digit with her other hand and darted to the basin, shrieking. "I can't do it—I can't. I need some miracle to happen." Tears dripped over her cheeks as she wailed, "please—please, I beg, my wedding dress must be perfect for morning."

Three loud cracks met the door. Sarah shuddered "who's there?"

"A friend. My name is Lucinda."

"But, who are you?"

"I've come to hasten your craft. Your sweet mother,

who I watched die giving birth to you, was my dearest friend."

"Come in" Sarah cried, throwing open the door. A wizened, wrinkled old woman shuffled in.

"Here it is my lovely" the crone made an unsuccessful attempt at a smile as she proffered a golden thimble. Sarah's heart pounded at the sight of the shining object. Slipping it on her finger, she witnessed the blister disappear leaving her sewing hand ready to resume her work. Wide eyed she whispered "what is your fee?"

A smirk licked the visitor's face. "No payment required, but it is not quite free of charge."

Sarah began to stitch. The needle slipped in and out appearing to work on its own accord. When dawn flickered through the window, the sun shone on an exquisite gown.

The wedding carriage arrived at the door. All was ready. A veil, decorated with intricate lace and pearls, hid the bride's face. She clung to the old woman and pleaded. "Will you give me away?"

"Oh yes, my lovely. But you must firstly return my thimble." Sarah handed over the object. Lucinda seized it and placed it on her own withered wedding ring finger humming the tune of a well-known lament.

Flowers trembled in the girl's grasp as she listened to the haunting words.

"All that glistens is not always gold
the magic thimble can never be sold
Remember your wish was not quite free
for I am now you and you will be me."

BEYOND
EXPECTATIONS

JANET CRAWFORD

Exactly where the noise came from she wasn't exactly sure. Without the ability to pinpoint it, having removed her charred ears - setting them aside for now along with her inhibitions - she was like every other masked clown... oblivious.

Then her synaesthesia took over, the gift for which she'd paid a hefty price, and she saw the brightness of the lightning forking slightly to her left. Her lips curved in a thin smile, splitting wider as the tip of her tongue hit the hard plastic mask she hid behind. She shuddered with a warming delight at the feel of her tongue against the cooling surface. A teaser of what was to come. Memories of long cooled skin rose within her. Wild horses couldn't stop her now, even those of long dead daughters.

She'd gone to a supermarket, following a group of excited shouty children closely, looking to search out a costume which would fit well amongst the guisers and drunken teenager who'd fill the streets tomorrow evening. The garishly bright face paints, plastic cats, tridents, and luminous witch hats had bemused her somewhat and until she saw the so called 'scream mask'- a silly name but it was how it had been advertised on the packaging- she'd thought she was wasting her time, after all midnight on Halloween only came once a year...

Her eyes shone brightly taking in the gathering gloom beyond the fading lightening fork and settled on the lone walker. Stiletto heels tip tapping, like a sos which would go unanswered on the cold grey paving, their wearers slightly tipsy gait meant there'd be little chance of running. Alcohol never let you down. Having given up counting, after the first five who'd let out no screams as she'd unmasked, Horne sidled up to the young woman, silently lifting her shadow feet from the footpath and wrapped her thin gauze cloak around them both. Witches never die... hadn't society learnt anything since 1727.

THE LAST EMAIL

MARGARET WALKER

I opened the carrier bag carefully and took out the red and black sparkly dress. I laid it out along the settee, its sequins brightly reflecting the autumn sunlight. How I had admired that dress when Joan showed me it last year. She had bought it for her son's wedding but declared she would NEVER wear it when the wedding had been cancelled a week before. I doubted that I would ever wear it either despite its fragile lace and chiffon beauty.

For the twentieth time since yesterday I crossed over to the computer and switched it on. "Right," I said, heart pounding, "let's check these dates again." Sure enough, there it was – Sunday 6.15pm my email to Joan.

"Hi there Joan, how are things? Sorry I've not been in touch for a while, time seems to fly. I wondered if I could ask a favour? Could I possibly borrow that gorgeous red dress you bought last year? I hope you don't mind my asking."

And there was Joan's reply – Sunday 6.20pm: "Hi Margaret. Thanks for your email, it's good to hear from you. Where are you? I don't quite know where I am at the moment. It is very peaceful here and I can see a really bright light far, far away in the distance, getting brighter as it comes closer." I was, of course, surprised by this reply.

Sunday 6.25pm: "Hi Joan, I am at home just now. Are you OK?" After a bit of thought I added, "I was hoping to borrow your dress to wear for Doug's company dinner-dance. It's on Halloween and it's quite a big affair, formal dress."

Sunday 6.30pm: "Of course you can have the dress. Come round whenever you like and take anything you want. I don't think I want those old clothes any more."

Well that was indeed a surprise. Joan was the trimmest, neatest most fashion conscious person I had ever met and her wardrobe was full of beautiful things which I know she loves. We are about the same size so her offer intrigued me. Why did she not want her clothes? Sunday 6.35pm: "Are you sure? Have you been on a diet or something? I will pop round tomorrow about lunchtime if that's OK."

Sunday 6.40pm: "That will be fine, I will look out that dress for you. But please Mags take away anything you fancy. I won't be needing any of that stuff."

I then sent a reply to the effect that I would see her tomorrow, switched off the computer, grabbed my bag and hurried out, I had my writing club that evening. As I locked the front door and walked down the path to the car, I noticed the sky glowing pink and golden from a beautiful sunset. And just above me, a goose flew by, honking loudly and looking incredibly lonely. I could see no sign of the flock so I hoped he would catch up with the others.

Well, there I was next day, about 12.00, ringing the bell to Joan's neat little bungalow. Her next-door neighbour appeared, she came right up to me and put her arm around my shoulder. "Margaret, I am so sorry to tell you the news. Joan passed away at the weekend."

"What? No, that can't be right, I heard from her last night."

She looked at me sadly. "I don't think that is possible. Her son found her yesterday, slumped over her computer keyboard. She was stone cold and had been dead for at least a day. Oh, but there was a bag with your name on it. I took it into my house, here it is." She handed me the carrier bag with the dress in it.

What was I to think?!

MISCHIEF
IN MUCKTON

SUSI J. SMITH

(The events in this short story take place six months after the first novel in the Murder in Moorbank series, Chocolate Cake and a Corpse)

"We're going on a ghost hunt." Mum stands in the kitchen doorway, applying a thick coat of baby pink lipstick.

"What are you wearing?"

She turns, letting me take in the whole ensemble. Her tousled cherry tresses clash with her neon green crop top. Below rests a snake-print mini skirt, and some dangerously high black heels.

"It's..." Words fail me. Polite ones, at least.

She poses, one hand on the doorframe, the other on her hip. "I'm a lady of the night."

Archibald stares at her from his basket in the corner, his head tilted. He looks as confused as I am. Finally, I ask,

"Why?"

Mum tuts. "It's my Halloween costume."

I envisage her running round Moorbank being chased by the local police. It wouldn't be the first time. I rather think she enjoys it. Perhaps that's her plan.

"Is that wise?"

She drops the pose. "Why wouldn't it be?"

Because it's indecent. Because you're sixty-eight. Because you have a reputation for being promiscuous. Because, considering each item of this outfit came straight out of your wardrobe, people might not realise it's a costume.

"Because parents aren't going to let their kids anywhere near you dressed like that." Well done, Nora, that had less sugar-coating than an avocado.

Marching over to the kettle she flicks the switch. "At least I made an effort, what are you supposed to be? A middle-aged frump?"

"I'm supposed to be studying, remember?"

She glances at the cover of my textbook. "'Anatomy and Physiology'. Bit technical for a bum wiper."

I deserve that. "So where are you off to?"

"You'll see." She hands me a cup of tea. "You'd best get changed before Matty gets here."

I frown. Mum frowns in response before her shoulders slump. "Nora, I told you."

"I don't remember, when did you tell me?"

"Just now, when I came into the kitchen." She slurps her tea. "So, have you decided on a costume?"

"In the last thirty seconds? Funnily enough, no, I

haven't."

She scoffs. "It's been at least a minute."

There's a brief knock before the front door rattles open. Archibald barks and trots over to greet Matty who bends down to clap him. Matty's wearing a Panama hat, and a cream frock coat over a vintage cricket outfit. A stick of celery is pinned to his lapel.

"Very handsome, Matty." It's a lot smarter than his normal ensemble.

He bows theatrically. "And you're... A librarian. Fantastic."

I blush, removing my reading glasses.

"Actually, Nora's still thinking what to wear. She's been too busy with her books." Mum gestures, slopping tea onto the floor.

Matty flicks through my textbook. "Found the naughty pictures yet?"

Giggling, Mum leans over my shoulder. Rolling my eyes, I pull the book away.

"Spoilsport." She straightens. "Grab yourself a drink, Matty. I'm just going to find a costume for Nora."

I jump to my feet. "What? No. I never said..."

Mum scurries from the room before I can stop her.

Matty squeezes my shoulder. "Brave heart, Nora." Pulling a hipflask from his coat, he offers it to me. I shake my head. It's barely gone ten am.

"I'll keep it handy, you might need it, knowing Marian." Pocketing the flask, he opens the fridge, helping himself to some leftover pasta. He doesn't seem to mind that it's cold. Nor does he bother with a fork, instead, tipping it directly from the bowl into his mouth.

Mum's back in minutes looking thoroughly amused with herself. "It's on your bed. Hurry up, we're going in five."

I look to Matty for support. He runs a finger round the inside of the bowl, ignoring my obvious plea for assistance. Taking a deep breath, I trudge up the stairs to my doom.

The bedroom door is open. Resting on the bed is a neat pile of clothes. They're less vibrant than I expected. In fact... I step closer, my hand brushing the soft fabric. They're mine.

Slipping into the exquisite black Karen Millen dress, I gaze at myself in the mirrored wardrobe door. The bags under my eyes speak of my recent hardship, and Mum's high-fat diet has taken its toll on my waistline, but other than that, it's as if I've stepped back into my old life.

"Like it?" Mum walks over.

I nod, unable to speak.

"I thought it was about time you got some use out of those fancy clothes of yours."

"What..."

She grins. "You're a socialite. Come on, before Matty eats us out of house and home."

Matty gives an appreciative whistle as I descend the stairs. Archibald sits at his feet, a pair of bat-wings fastened to his back. What else has Matty got hidden in that coat of his?

We clamber into Mum's yellow three-door Mini, Matty folding his long legs to squeeze into the back.

I really hope Mum isn't setting me up. It wouldn't be the first time. And Matty may look like a dishevelled angel, but he's no better. But then, he is a solicitor.

It must be a trick. Who goes ghost hunting in broad daylight? Unless it's a family-friendly event... Oh, no, please don't be at the church. Not again.

"Where are we going?" Fastening my seatbelt, I lift Archibald onto my lap.

"The old abandoned psychiatric hospital."

Phew!

Mum cackles loudly as the car screeches out of the driveway.

"I thought you were a lady of the night, not a witch."

She glares at me. "I can be both."

The hospital is situated in the neighbouring town of Muckton, surrounded by dense woodland. Paths lead between the main hospital and the rest of the expansive site which comprises administration buildings, villas, a shop, and even a small railway.

Parking next to a metal barrier, we climb out and are greeted by a 'no trespassing' sign. Normally such a notice would have me locking myself in the car, refusing to be drawn into another of Mum's ridiculous schemes. However, the sign has long been ignored by the nearby residents. Many dog walkers use the site, including myself.

An icy breeze prickles my legs. Mum must be freezing, not that she's show it. I clip Archibald's lead onto his collar and follow them round the barrier and up the path to the first building — the shop. Matty pulls an old 35mm camera from his pocket and hands it to Mum, before offering me a digital recorder produced from another pocket. What it going on with that coat?

Grudgingly accepting the device, I look around, expecting to see other costume-clad people milling about, waiting for the ghost hunt to begin. Instead, all I see are looks of confusion and horror on the faces of passersby.

I groan. What have I been tricked into this time? Still, at least I'm not the one dressed as a—

"It is here..." Matty stands outside the shop, his arms spread wide. "That the ghost of wee Bessie Malone has been seen. Some say—"

"Wheesht you! This isn't one of those daft American reality shows, this is serious." Mum trudges up the hill towards the main hospital, her heels clicking on the concrete. With a shrug, Matty, Archibald, and I traipse after her.

MDF panels line the inside of the windows, they're badly fitted, leaving gaps through which the inside of the building is just about visible. Mum pulls at the boards on the front door. The nails hold fast. She turns to Matty. "Hypothetically, say I just so happened to have a crowbar, where would we stand legally if I... loosened these."

"Hypothetically?" He suppresses a grin. "And where would you have obtained this hypothetical crowbar?"

"I have hypothetical contacts."

They share a look. The atmosphere suddenly uncomfortable, I clear my throat and I kneel to ruffle Archibald's fur.

Matty suppresses a grin. "Housebreaking is—"

"This isn't a house," she indicates the building. "It's a

hospital."

He nods, considering. "That's true."

Please tell me he's not going to condone this.

"But trespassing, of any type of building, is a delict—
"

Mum sighs. "In English, Matty."

"Usually we're talking a £200 fine, but with your record..." He glances at me, uncertainly.

I feign shock. "She has a record? You do surprise me."

There's a loud creak and a crack. Mum stands beside a broken board. "It came off in my hand, must be rotten." She vanishes from sight, Matty hurries after her. Archibald and I stay outside.

She's up to something.

I inspect the board. The break is fresh, the wood hard. Behind the panel, tucked out of sight, lies a crowbar. Where did she... Sighing, I tug Archibald's lead, directing him to follow.

Debris from the partially caved in ceiling litters the floor. A fluorescent light hangs down. Just visible through an arched doorway lies a mortuary trolley.

"I think we should head back to the path, security will be by soon."

Matty and Mum ignore me, they walk round the room moving about rubble and whispering. I clear my throat loudly. Still, they take no notice. Archibald barks, tugging at his leash. Mum frowns at him. "Let him off, I think he smells something."

"Absolutely not." I pick him up.

She scoffs. "Fine, then make yourself useful."

"How, exactly?"

"Ask the ghosts questions, of course."

Of course. I switch on the digital recorder but can't bring myself to ask questions. Mum and Matty, on the other hand, appear to be well-acquainted with this bizarre pursuit, Matty checking the temperature in different parts of the room, Mum snapping pictures when instructed.

Archibald growls, his teeth bared. I follow his gaze. Nothing. But still he stares.

Mum's camera flashes, momentarily blinding me. With a sudden bark, Archibald leaps from my arms and bounds out of the room.

"Archibald!" I hurry after him, the floorboards bending underfoot. Cobwebs cling to my face as I push the mortuary trolley aside and stand in the corridor beyond. Doors line the walls. The roof has long since given in and hangs in broken beams. Metal scaffolding props up the remnants.

A whimper echoes in the barren building. Mum and Matty rush to my side.

"Which way did he go?" Matty looks left and right.

"I didn't see. Archibald?" My voice ricochets.

Mum puts her arm around me. "We'll find him."

A whine answers my whistle, the sound difficult to trace. "I think he's hurt."

Matty strides forward, heading left. With a sudden yell, he drops to the ground about thirty metres from us.

"Matty?" Mum taps her way over, kneeling beside him.

Swearing under his breath, Matty frees his foot from the broken floorboards, his trousers torn. "It's rotten." He inspects the cut on his ankle. "We should head back."

"No, I'm not leaving him." My body kept as close to the walls as the roof fragments allow, I edge further into the hospital, my feet shuffling as I tentatively check the floor will take my weight.

Archibald barks. The noise is coming from a door across the corridor. Hitching up my dress, I commando crawl over the dust-coated floor. Plaster, and wood splinters scrape my skin. The pain too much, I climb to my feet but keep my hands on the ground, trying to distribute my weight.

A bright light flashes. Mum stands a few feet back, photographing my rescue efforts.

"I thought you might like to remember this magical moment." She looks at the image, grinning. "I certainly will."

I wave a hand at her. "Get down."

"In this skirt? No chance."

I roll my eyes.

"You'll go blind doing that."

No, no I won't.

Dust tickles my nose, splinters prick my palms. Finally, I reach the room. Inside lies a rusty metal bed frame, shredded fabric, and further detritus. Crude graffiti colours the walls. Archibald cowers in a corner, his ears low, his tail tucked tightly between his legs, his eyes fixed on the large rat in front of him.

"Shoo." I wave at the rodent. It ignores me. I stick my

head back into the corridor. "Any idea how to get rid of a rat?"

"Oh, so now you want my dating advice."

I roll my eyes again.

"I saw that." Mum totters over and peers in the room. "Hang on." She taps away on her mobile. "It says they don't like ammonia. Do we have any of that?"

I make a pretence of patting down my dress. "Must have left it in my other costume."

She considers. "We could pee on it."

"How exactly?" I can't believe I'm even asking.

"Well... Hang on." She trots back down the corridor. Please don't let her be planning what I think she's planning.

I shuffle nearer, waving my hand. The rat turns, its beady eyes trained on me, its tail swishing back and forth. I'm no expert in rat behaviour, but I don't think it's best pleased.

There's a shout. A high heel batters to the ground next to the rat. It scurries off, squeaking. Mum leans against the doorframe, balancing on one foot.

Archibald yips and jumps into my arms. I run my hand over him. His ear's bleeding, but it doesn't look serious.

Mum limps after her shoe.

"Thanks, Mum." I cuddle Archibald. "For a second there, I thought you were going to ask Matty to... You know."

"Me? Never." She slips her stiletto on. "Besides, he refused." She raises her voice for the last part, no doubt to get a rise from her friend. It works. Matty's voice resonates in response. "I told you, I don't need. Besides, how good do you think my aim is? It's not like I practice."

"Who's he's kidding? All men practice that." Mum helps me to my feet and we shuffle back to the entrance, Matty hobbling after us.

Squeezing out the gap, we are greeted by a dark grey car with flashing blue lights emitting from its grille. DI Andrew Buchanan stands, crowbar in hand.

"When I say run..." Matty whispers.

"Miss James, Mr Pender, and Mrs McIntyre, what a surprise."

Buchanan doesn't look in the least surprised. Admittedly, if I were him, I wouldn't be surprised either.

He continues. "What brings you here?"

Mum answers before I have a chance to stop her. "I could ask you the same thing."

"I'm assisting with the patrols. And you?"

She sighs. "We're taking Archibald for a walk. Is that a crime?"

"No, it isn't." His gaze sweeps over her costume. "That's a very... interesting outfit, Miss James."

Mum strikes a pose. "I'm a lady of—"

"Fashion." I glare at her. She meets my eye. "The night." Her face is smug.

Buchanan cocks an eyebrow. "Is that so?"

Matty clears his throat and shambles forward. "Allow me to clarify, for the official record. What my client means to say is—"

"Exactly what I said. I'm not senile."

No, just insane. She does remember he's a policeman, doesn't she? Surely the flashing blue lights are a rather obvious clue.

Matty giggles nervously before clearing his throat again. "It's a costume, my client is not... has never... Care for a Jelly Baby?" He pulls a crumpled packet from his pocket.

Seriously, what is going on with that coat?

Mum places her hands on her hips. "Are you planning to arrest me for solicitation?"

Buchanan shakes his head. "Not at this time."

"Good." Mum takes hold of Matty's arm.

"Tell me..." Buchanan inspects the crowbar. "Do you usually walk Archibald inside derelict buildings?"

"Kids." She looks in the direction of the broken board. "Poor Archibald chased a rat into the building. We were just getting him back out safely."

That's... very plausible.

Buchanan pouts, considering. "So, you weren't engaging in housebreaking?"

"It's not a house," she gestures at the building. "It's a hospital."

"Regardless—"

"Regardless, unless you plan on pressing charges against my client, I will assume that we are free to go." Matty doffs his hat and we assist him towards the car.

"Miss James..." Buchanan holds up the crowbar. "You forgot something."

She scoffs. "That's not mine."

"Really, because it's inscribed."

It is? Who gives a crowbar as a gift?

"'To Marian, thanks for giving me a chance, love Matty'."

I groan. Hypothetical contacts indeed.

Mum shrugs. "Could be anyone's."

"Circumstantial evidence." Matty interjects. "My client could have left that here at any time. However, as it is clearly hers..." He holds out a hand. Buchanan allows him to take hold of the crowbar but doesn't relinquish his grip, his eyes fixed on Mum.

"Tread lightly, Miss James." He releases the crowbar.

When we're finally back in the car, I breathe a sigh of relief. "You could have got us in a lot of trouble there."

"Don't blame Matty, he did his best."

"I wasn't blaming Matty."

"Ladies please, there's no need to fight over me." Matty grins. "There's enough of me to go around."

"Nonsense, there's not a pick on you." Mum hands him the camera. I pass him the digital recorder, it's still running. Matty hits rewind. "Might have got some good stuff on this."

"Yes, like Mum suggesting we pee on a rat."

"Might have worked that."

I glower at her. "We'll never know."

"Speak for yourself."

Shuffling steps emanate from the recorder. Mum and Matty lock eyes. I sigh. "That's just me negotiating the rotten floorboards."

Archibald growls, baring his teeth.

"And that?" Mum snatches the recorder.

"Maybe he hears the rat on it."

"Are you the nurse?" The voice is clear, young, female.

Throwing the recorder back at Matty, Mum starts the car and speeds off back towards home.

The End

THE ASH GROVE
AT HALLOWEEN

COLIN MITCHELL

Down yonder green valley, where streamlets meandered,
When twilight was fading, to pensively rove
That Hallowe'en nightfall I solemnly wandered,
Amid the dark shades of the lonely ash grove;
'Twas there that I met it, the foulest fiend I'd seen
With three red eyes glowing, and stench on its breath
All round me the shadows, where daylight had once been
The air cold as ice and foretelling of death
Gripped with fear, I stood there and felt the blood draining
From my face and seeming to cover the ground
The beast then turned to me; its fangs were all raining
Saliva which burned through the leaves that it found
It had come to seek my soul in this darkening gloaming
I felt its breath o'er me, a pain in my chest
And now those who wander, or come this way roaming
Walk over the place where my body's at rest.

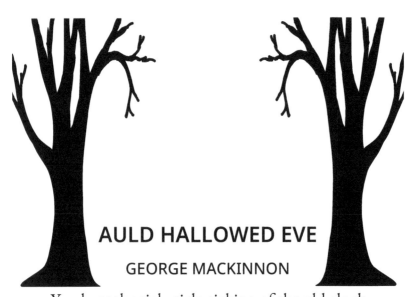

AULD HALLOWED EVE

GEORGE MACKINNON

You hear the tick, tick, ticking of the old clock
As the sound of the wind hollows outside
And you hear creaks from the old house
As it braces itself for the night to come
While inside... the chill from the outside
Breaks the warmth of the fire
Curtains rustle from the cracks
Around the window frames
Sending a cool shiver down your back
Footsteps echo... from along the hallway
But nobody is there
Thumps go bang... from up the stairs
As the hairs upon the back of your neck
Rise up at the thought of what is out there...
The sound of voices... start to play in the mind

As the darkness slowly creeps
Its way into where you now sit...
Evil lurks within the darkest corners of the house
As all the ghosts, spirits and the ghouls
Of auld Hallowed Eve, start to come out to play
As shadows cast long fingers from nearby trees
Screams, moans and weird noises join in with the
melodies... casting unwanted images upon the mind
Tonight is going to be a long night
One of sleep deprivation
Which will unnerve you very soul
And then... when morning comes
You will wonder why you felt so ill at ease

GEORGE THE
DEPRESSED GHOST

ROBERT ARCHIBALD

"Our next act is new to the comedy scene so make him feel at home," the emcee said.

"What, nag him incessantly and call him a useless good for nothing?" someone shouted from the small audience, getting a few laughs for his effort.

"Gentlemen, and that one lady who missed the bingo and came in here by mistake, I give you George Cornley!"

The emcee walked off the stage, hands held aloft trying to encourage at least a smattering of polite applause. At the same time, from the other wing, another man bounded onto the stage. He was of medium height but overweight making him look like a giant egg, or one of those inflatable dolls designed to be continually knocked over but always bounce back upright. His hair was straggly, perfectly matching the beard and moustache. Beneath the stage light beads of sweat were already visible across his brow.

"Good evening!" he cried when he reached the microphone. There was a shrill of feedback which caused him to wince. Lowering his voice slightly, he said, "So, as everyone knows, Halloween is just around the corner which makes me think about ghosts and what life must be like for them." He paused as if waiting for laughter but was greeted with silence. "You know, life? Coz, well, ghosts are dead, right?" He chuckled nervously as the silence pervaded. "Um, anyway, it's a little known fact about ghosts that, actually, they eat and drink, yeah? But it's a very particular diet they have; they can only eat ghoul-ash and drink spirits!" He smiled nervously and tapped the microphone. "Is this thing switched on?" Another nervous chuckle. "And, er, when it's raining, of course, they'll most likely wear a ca-ghoul!"

A smattering of boos filled the air.

"Oh, thank God!" George said. "I was starting to think there was nobody here."

"There won't be soon, mate, if you keep that up!" someone shouted, earning a burst of applause.

George shaded his eyes from the stage light and saw a man walking up the aisle toward the exit.

"Wait, don't go!" George cried, trying not to wince at the desperation in his voice. "I'm... I'm just getting warmed up."

The man, a dark silhouette, stopped and turned around. "Warmed up?" he heckled. "I've met warmer corpses!"

As the audience laughed some more, George had to

admit the heckler was good. Still, he was determined not to go down without a fight. Metaphorically speaking, at any rate.

"Where you going?" he asked. "You sure you want to miss out on the fun?"

"Fun?" the man retorted. "That's your best joke yet! Anyway, it'll be closing time soon. I thought I might go and pick a fight with a big, angry drunk. At least that way there's a chance I'll end up in stitches!"

The laughter increased in intensity as George opened and closed his mouth, unable to come up with a suitable retort. Then the pain seized him, like a weight crushing his chest...

"And you know, when I look back on it, that was the best time of my life." George lay back on the couch.

"George, you died on that stage, in every sense. I mean, quite literally, you passed away," the woman sitting beside the couch, notepad in hand, pen poised, told him.

"I know, Dr Spook, but still," George said. "I was living the dream, wasn't I?" He sounded wistful. "There's nothing quite like the rush you get once you're on that stage, just you and your verbal wits to entertain the baying mob."

Dr Spook brushed a strand of silver hair from her face. Black-framed glasses magnified her green eyes, made her lashes look bigger, too, and seemed to stand out sharply against her pale skin. The merest hint of lipstick highlighted her mouth, currently puckered in thought.

She studied her notes though, truthfully, after so many sessions with George, she did not need to.

"George, that was your first attempt at stand-up, am I correct?"

"Well, if you want to be particular about it." George sounded peeved.

"My point is, you seem fixated on this idea that you were, well, some sort of success," Dr Spook said, not for the first time.

"I know, I know!" George spoke quickly. "But I know I could have been a success, I'm sure of it!"

"George, your heckler got more laughs than you."

"I was... I was just, um, getting started," George replied, not sounding convincing.

"You know, as a ghost, I should probably find your material offensive," Dr Spook observed with a slight smile.

"That's where I went wrong." George snapped his fingers. "I should have been more... more edgy. Controversial. That would have been the way to go. I could've been cancelled!"

"I suspect if you had continued your act, all future bookings would have been cancelled."

"Oh, ha, ha, everyone's a comedian."

"Sadly not everyone," the doctor noted wryly.

"But I didn't get to the best jokes," George whined. "Like, why can a ghost be both mother and father? Because they're trans-parent! Get it? That would've got me cancelled for sure."

"George, please stop. Right now." Dr Spook rolled

her eyes and held her hands up. "It's been, what, twenty years since you died. You're still having trouble adjusting, I understand that. Dying is quite a big step."

"Oh, I know, we've talked about this." George sighed.

"And we can keep talking it over, as many times as you need." Dr Spook offered him an encouraging smile. "My job is to help you adjust. It doesn't matter how many sessions you need, either."

"I think that's part of the problem," George told her.

"How so?"

"Well, I know it's only been twenty years but I already feel like I'm stuck in a rut." George lay back and stared at the office ceiling. "I mean, do you ever wonder what the point of everything is?"

"A purpose?" Dr Spook asked.

"Oh, I dunno." George sighed again. "Sure, there's all the hauntings, especially at this time of year. But, is that all there is? Isn't there more to the afterlife?"

"It's natural you feel maudlin at this time of year, the time when you died," Dr Spook said. "Some people celebrate their death day, others don't like to dwell on how long they've been dead. You'd be surprised how many ghosts are only twenty-one years' dead!" She laughed. "But for a lot of us, it is a time to think about where we came from, where we're going. It's perfectly normal."

"But what's the point?" George asked. "What is the meaning of the afterlife?"

"That's quite a philosophical question, George." Dr Spook placed her notepad down. "It's a question I can't answer for you. For some, simply searching for the answer is enough to keep them going. Others are happy just being able to carry out their hauntings."

George frowned, puzzled. "You think I can find meaning in striving to find meaning?"

Dr Spook shrugged her shoulders. "Tell me, George, what if there was no meaning?"

"I don't understand."

"What if you're simply overthinking things?" Dr Spook continued. "What if there is no answer?"

"Aren't you supposed to be helping me, doctor?" George muttered.

"My point," Dr Spook said with a smile, "is; answer or no answer, ultimately it can be whatever you choose it to be."

"I'm not convinced." George frowned.

"Okay, George, our time is almost up," Dr Spook announced. "Here's what I want you to do. Go to roll-call, collect your assignment and carry it out. Think only about your assignment and nothing else. Be totally in the moment. Can you do that? Maybe the answer will come to you when you're not fixated on the question. Maybe not. Either way, try it and, next time, we can discuss how you felt. Okay?"

The roll-call room appeared to be about the size of a standard classroom although it never seemed to have trouble accommodating the multitude of ghosts who attended. At the head of the room, behind a small podium, a tall, lean man called out a series of names.

Clearing his throat, looking doubtful, he said, "Wee Gadgie."

Beside George, a young man spoke excitedly. "Aw, ye wee dancer. That's me!" He waved a Burberry cap in the air as he hurried up to the podium and was passed a sheet of paper. Returning to his spot beside George, he read the sheet of paper, grinning broadly.

"Oh, ye beauty, a Level 3, proper scare-the-pants-aff-the-bugger haunting!" he told George.

George wondered how Wee Gadgie could already by getting Level 3 assignments.

"Erm, a good one, is it?" George asked.

"Oh, aye!" Wee Gadgie replied. He scanned the paper some more. "Better 'n better," he murmured. "The auld biddy has a pacemaker. I could get a heart attack oot o' this!" He looked at George. "Oh, sorry, big man, that's how you went, isn't it? Nae offence, like. Onyway, there's a wee dug, tae. Dae ah get bonus points if ah make the dug shite itsel'?"

George noticed the bottle sticking out of Wee Gadgie's jacket. Buckfast. Not a tipple George was familiar with, if he was honest. Probably just as well if it turned you into... into... whatever Wee Gadgie was. Still, with his bloodshot eyes and indecipherable mutterings, George supposed Wee Gadgie would be a natural at Level 3.

Whoever the poor woman was, George thought, she'll most certainly get a fright. Doug, too, whoever he was.

"Whit aboot you?" Wee Gadgie asked, looking at the sheet of paper George was holding.

"Oh, erm, another Level 1," George murmured, embarrassed.

"Nothin' wrang wi' a Level Wan," Wee Gadgie said. "It's no' everyone who kin be, like, sneaky enough t' move things aboot, jist ever so, like, bit enough t' unsettle the bampot, ken?"

George was not entirely sure, but he thought the young man was trying to offer him words of encouragement. And did he just call him Ken?

If only he spoke English.

"Okay," announced the man at the podium. "Everyone has their assignments. Let's make this the scariest Halloween yet!"

George left, silently bemoaning the fact he had heard the same thing twenty times now. And the fact he had still not plucked up the courage to tell Dr Spook about his biggest problem...

A Level 1 assignment was considered one of the more basic hauntings. In this instance, George was to visit a suburban detached house. Everything fairly run of the mill, parents, two children, pet dog, two cars sitting in front of the single garage. George was yet to learn how the assignments came to be. Was there some kind of phone number or website people could visit to request a haunting? Maybe a higher power decided, using them as a way to keep the deceased busy.

Another sigh, an affectation George retained from his life. It seemed to be the thing he did most often, the thing which perfectly encapsulated how he felt, so it was hardly surprising George continued this. Even though he did not breathe, he clung to the idea of sighing. If he lost even that, he was not sure he would be able to go on.

George glanced at the small sheet of paper. Float in, nudge a couple of ornaments, maybe knock something off a shelf, run a chill up the adults' spines as they sat in bed reading.

Looking down on the house, George hmm'd and haw'd to himself. When he could put it off no longer, he allowed himself to drift down until he found himself passing through brick and concrete, dropping into the living room. Directly in front of him was the mantle-piece decorated with a row of tiny figurines made from fine china.

George approached them and raised a hand out to the nearest one concentrated. For all ghosts, this was the simplest of tasks, something which seemed to come nat-urally to them. Unfortunately, George still struggled with this, much to his embarrassment. He scrunched his eyes together, teeth gritted as he tried to will the ornament to move. He reached the point where he felt he may have in-duced an aneurysm if he had still been alive when the fig-urine wobbled ever so slightly. Renewing his efforts, George strained as hard as he possibly could.

The sound of his fart startled him and made him lose his focus. He had strained so hard, he realised, that, well, he was thankful, really, that he wasn't alive.

The sound of the dog's bark made him jump. A small dog, some kind of terrier, bounded into the room yipping excitedly, running circles around George.

It is a little known fact about spectral farts that sometimes animals can hear them. Could they smell them? George wondered. And would he ever be brave enough to speak with Dr Spook about this problem?

Seconds later, the sound of footsteps descending the stairs were quickly followed by a light clicking on and George found himself staring at the two adults.

"Samson! Shush!" the man, dressed in pyjamas, whispered sharply. "You'll wake up the entire street. Bad boy!"

Standing behind the man was his wife, leaning over his shoulder, eyes looking around.

"Geoffrey," she said softly, "be careful."

"There's nobody here, Pamela," Geoffrey muttered. "See for yourself."

Pamela stepped around and, tightening the sash on her dressing gown, took in the room. "I thought I heard something," she said, uncertainty clouding her face.

"Is anything missing?" Geoffrey asked.

"No, I don't think-"

"And, my God, what is that stench?" Geoffrey glared at Samson. "You better not have pooh-poohed or Daddy will be most unamused."

Samson ignored his master and continued to run circles around George, sniffling and growling.

"The smell's only in here." Pamela wrinkled her nose. "There's no mess, Geoffrey. Do you think Samson, well, you know?" she asked.

"You can say 'farted', Pamela," Geoffrey snapped. "It won't lower the property value."

"There's no need to be sniffy!" Pamela retorted.

"Right now, I would gladly be anything but!" Geoffrey, satisfied that there was no intruder, added, "We're changing Samson's diet. Tomorrow! For something which won't... disagree with him. Come on, let's get back to bed. Samson, heel."

The light was turned off, and they headed back to the stairs, Samson running past them. Feeling despondent and completely useless, George decided it would be best if he left. As the wave of depression enveloped him, he drifted through the wall where the mantle-piece stood.

Unseen by George, as his form passed through the wall, several ornaments in his path all wobbled simultaneously, dancing across the narrow shelf and falling onto the floor, a couple smashing into smaller pieces.

Pamela let out a shriek and the next ten minutes was spent with the couple arguing about who should go back into the living room to check for intruders.

George returned to a cacophony of voices as everyone talked about their assignments. Excited chatter, peals of laughter, the same scene which had greeted him every time over the last twenty years. It seemed impossible to avoid the gathering and, sooner or later, someone would ask him how his assignment went. In the past, he had tried to avoid this part, but it seemed the more reluctant he was to speak about it, the more determined others were to hear the grisly details. Never comfortable talking about what he viewed as embarrassing failures, George tended to... embellish. The trick was to provide just enough details to match his assignment, perhaps with an extra bit thrown in here or there, but not go too far.

Realism was the key.

Reaching that conclusion was the last time George had managed even a half-hearted chuckle, if only for the irony of it.

"And then," a woman's voice said, "I just blew softly against his hair and, well, it was like he'd seen a ghost." There was a soft, overly polite chuckle from her as she finished.

"That's nothin! Ah swear to God," Wee Gadgie's voice reached George's ears, "ma yin wis this close to drappin' deid on the spot! She got such a fright she spat her falsers oot, let oot a scream that wid deefin' a banshee, then pished hersel' whaur she stood!" He laughed. "Ah reckon if ah'd pit in a wee bit mair effort, ah coulda made her shite hersel' tae! Aw, man, ah havnae laughed so hard in ages, like. If ah wis still alive, ah reckon ah'd have pished masel' tae! And as fir the dug, my God, it wis cooerin' and whimperin' and a' thing!"

George felt grateful he hardly understood a word Wee Gadgie said.

"Oh, hey, George, pal, hoo's it wi' you?" Wee Gadgie appeared beside George. "Go oan, then, big man, tell us hoo ye did." Wee Gadgie put an arm around George's shoulders. "Whit wis it, then? Did ye get the wifie to scream like a little girl? Wis the husband greetin' fir his mammy, like a wean? Come oan, man, dinnae keep me in suspense, like. But I bet ye cannae top ma night!"

Inwardly, George sighed.

SENGA'S HALLOWEEN

ERIC MCFARLANE

I was really tired when I got home. Had run all the way from the doctors because I thought Easty was on and then remembered I hadn't changed my watch so I'd missed it which explained that receptionist who has an attitude problem. She had no right to say that about my feet.

So when I got home I opened the door expecting to have a cup of tea and a wee lie down, when sweet Polly Perkins there's a mouldering mummy sitting on my sofa. It was all covered in these filthy, ragged bandages with pus or something oozing from its nose. It stood up and came shambling towards me, hands up, pus dripping onto the carpet and making this moaning noise. I wasn't having none of it.

"Senga, you are not funny," I said. "You think you are, but you're not."

Now I've got a sense of humour. Everyone laughs

when I tell a joke, but I was not in the mood for Senga's dressing up. She did it last year too, put on this stupid witch's costume with a pointy hat and silver moons and stars. Nothing wrong with that, but then she set up her cauldron. She put a big black pot on one of them camping stoves and filled it with water then when it boiled she threw in all sorts of stuff including some dead spiders she said she found under my bed, which she did not 'cos I clean under there regular as I do not like spiders ever since my boyfriend Stan, who were my first boyfriend when I was teens, put one in my teacup and it sank instead of floating and I didn't see it until I'd finished my tea. I got my own back on Stan 'cos I was sick all over his Aran jumper and as I'd been eating a cream cake with my tea, it were a little messy.

Anyways, this cauldron boiled and bubbled and she threw in some red dye and then some joke severed hands and feet what she got from Lidl's. It were really disgusting. "Just wait for the trick or treaters tonight, love, eh?" she cackled.

I had a bad feeling about it when two little girls in white sheets knocked on the door later on and Senga invited them in.

"Hello my lovelies, and what can Granny Bonegrinder do for you tonight?" all husky-voiced.

One girl stepped forward and said, "Please do you have any treats?"

"All my treats are in this here cauldron," she said as she stirred it. "Why don't you come closer and take a look?"

Well, they did, which were brave of them, and when they were near, Senga sticks her arm in, pulls out one of the joke hands and waves the thing in their faces. As you can imagine, they were out that door faster than a lollipop man could shake his stick, all screaming and all.

"Senga, I don't think you should have done that," I said. "Them poor little girlies."

Then the door opens again and there's a woman standing there looking a bit annoyed. I knew it must be their Mam what had been waiting outside.

"What happened here? What have you been doing?" she says, all pompous and staring at me.

I shook my head and pointed at Senga and made a witch's hat shape with my hands.

Before the woman could speak, Senga sticks out her hand to shake. "Madam Bonegrinder at your service."

Then the woman grabs Senga's hand, and it comes straight off, and she's left holding a bloody hand. It were so realistic that I screamed even though I realised Senga had stuffed one of the Lidl hands up her sleeve. There was a bone sticking out the back, and it were all bloody and dripping from the cauldron. Well, I thought that woman was having a heart attack. She drops the hand and lets out a shriek fit to raise the devil and staggers out the door rubbing her chest. Senga's laughing so much she reverses into the cauldron and knocks it flying and the fake blood and body bits and spiders go all over our carpet.

"Oops," says Senga.

We needed a new carpet, and I didn't speak to her for days after that. So you can see that Senga and Halloween are not a good mix, which was why I were so annoyed at her for dressing in the mummy costume.

She was right in front, towering over me like a carrot over a bean or a pea. Must have been wearing her heels.

Moan, moan, moan.

"Do you see the mess you're making? You can just go to your room and get that stupid costume off." I gave her a shove, and she shuffled backwards.

Moan?

"Go on, get to your room." I walked straight at her with my scowly face on. She backed into her room and I slammed the door shut. "And don't come out until you're decent. And you can clear up this yucky mess."

It's not like me, I know, but it had been such a bad day and she had just invoked me one step too far.

I plonked myself down on the sofa avoiding all the gooey bits and closed my eyes for a second, then the front door opened.

"Hello love. How's you?"

I stared at Senga as she bustled in.

"Been down the deli for some bratwurst. I'll make dinner tonight. You look as white as a sheet."

"Um," I said as she dropped her bag on the table.

"Just going to me room for a ciggy then I'll get started." She headed towards her bedroom.

"Erm," I said.

"Take a couple aspirin luv. Always helps me."

"I..." I began, but her bedroom door slammed shut and there was silence. Deep, deep silence.

It's been like that for the last hour and a half and I don't know what to do. I knocked on her door, but nobody said nothing. I could just open it and go in, but Senga likes her privates. I could dial 999, but I don't know what to say. Actually, I think I'll go down the pub for a wee glass. Maybe it will all be sorted when I get back.

LIGHTHOUSES

MARGARET WALKER

What do ye think of, city dwellers and country lovers, when ye look out to sea? Perhaps you think only of peace and quiet, waves gently lapping the shore as you eat your picnic on a sandy beach, sunlight silvering the far horizon. Or perhaps you think of wild storms; sea crashing over the pier, gulls screaming. Then, you may well consider lighthouses. You may even be watching from afar as the lighthouse winks its yellow eye. Turning, turning – now you see it, now you don't.

For many years past, mine has been the hand that turned the lantern; kept the wick trimmed; watched over the lives and safety of ships and their passengers. Alas, no more – my peace of mind has been destroyed. I write these words whilst I scan the horizon, waiting and praying for the supply ship, already two days overdue.

It all began some months ago, when my companion and fellow lighthouse keeper, James, was due to retire. For many years he had been employed by the Northern

Lighthouse Board and over the time we had worked together James and I had built up a firm friendship and working relationship. The loneliness and solitude of this job is not for everyone so a good companion is a boon. When we received word that James' successor had been found, we were pleased. To think, now, we actually joked and laughed at how apt his name is – Henry Seagull! The new lighthouse keeper. And, truth to say, when Henry Seagull arrived nothing seemed amiss. He was a small, thin individual with a restless, nervy demeanour. Behind wire-framed glasses, his eyes were as grey as a winter sea.

At first things went well, until, a few weeks into his tenure, our regular boat arrived with supplies to keep us going over the next few months, as winter fast approached. That was when it happened: the violin-case was carefully handed to Mr Seagull. His eyes sparkled, and he laughed gleefully as though meeting an old friend.

I have no real taste for music: the cries of gulls; the sweet, melodious fluting of curlews and oystercatchers; the eerie, sad songs of seals are all the music I care for. Perhaps, indeed, if Henry Seagull could have actually played the instrument, my torment at the noise might have lessened. But the cacophony he made sounded like a million cats being boiled alive.

Gradually, however, tunes began to emerge from the noise. Tunes no-one had ever before written or heard: evil-sounding chords, wild melodies, repeated over and over.

My ears rang and my head ached. Night after night he

played. I could get no sleep or peace. All that was bad enough, but what did awaken me one night was not the noise, but the unusual silence. Total quiet. No wind, no roar of the sea – no sound of the foghorn!

Sleepy no more, I arose, pulled on a coat and gazed through the window. The Haar is an eerie sea-fog, and it was all around us cloaking the rocks in thick grey swirling mist. As fast as I could, I hurried upstairs to the tower.

"What's happening – why is the horn not sounding?" I cried. He shot me a look of pure malice but did not move. I headed to the switch and pushed it. Immediately the friendly boom started.

We stood apart, saying nothing, his sea-grey eyes glaring at me from behind his glasses. I began to understand. I had heard tales of lighthouse keepers going insane. Or perhaps he had always been unhinged and the solitude and relentless noise of the ocean had driven him over the edge. Yet, I could pity him for who knew what storms in life had buffeted him, his mind and his soul?

He alone now wields power over life and death. I know what will come next. The light extinguished. With no beam to warn them, ships will founder on our rocks. Men will drown whilst he plays his mad melodies.

And for myself – what will happen to me! As I write, I am in the comparative safety of a tiny shed attached to the main building. If (when) he traces me to my hiding place, I have ropes ready - ready to lash myself to the furthermost rock. I pray to God I will be rescued in time. Even at this moment I can hear the sound of his violin. But when that stops...

MASKING THE TRUTH
A JIM AND JOSH
STORY

EVIE JOHNSTONE

The outer door crashed open, smacking hard against a wall of meticulously arranged posters. 'Lost', 'Wanted' and 'Done the crime. Do the time' fluttered to the floor. Behind his front counter, the police sergeant took one look at the wild-eyed woman in the doorway and lifted his phone to ring upstairs for reinforcements.

As his call connected with the CID room, the new arrival clapped her hand to her head, wailed and sank out of sight.

Aw hell, thought the officer, that's a' ah need! and he disconnected the call.

The woman was lying half in and half out of the door. She was wearing a smart navy suit but one shoe was missing and her make up and hair were in total disarray. He knelt beside her, placed two fingers to her neck. "At least there's a pulse." He tapped her, none too gently, on the cheek. Her eyes fluttered open. She focused, tried to sit up. Croaked "I've just seen my husband," and closed her eyes again.

Struggling to his feet, he picked up the internal phone and re-dialled the number.

A voice answered immediately sounding slightly puzzled. "D.C. Laidlaw here. All right down there, sir?"

"It's Sergeant Price," he said. "Can someone come down and deal with a woman at the front counter?" He shook his head. "Always better to be economical with the facts in these situations."

After a few moments, feet on the stair heralded the arrival of the D.C. He pushed open the door to the front area and looked around the room. "A woman," he queried, lifting his eyebrows. "Has she gone?"

Sergeant Price pointed over his counter and the detective followed his direction.

"Jeezus, Mary an... "

"Naw son," answered the sergeant, heartily sick of that line. "Ah can assure you that this is not Jesus. Can ye get her out of my front office please? Put her in the interview room and make her a cup of tea!"

***

The door to Meeting Room 2 was ajar, Josh noticed as he was making his way to the mess room. Handler and dog had been on a drug raid since the early hours. A break was well overdue. As he passed the glass wall, he could see several people seated, listening to one man standing by the white board.

"Wonder if that's the new D.I." He spoke absently to his dog – as all police handlers do – "Barr? D.I. Barr." His hand was stretching out for the door marked Kitchen when a voice made him jump.

"Get tha' sel in 'ere lad an' bring t' mutt!"

Josh patted his thigh, and the dog stood quietly at his side. Then he looked over his shoulder to see who had spoken. The overall impression was brown. Brown pullover, brown corduroy trousers and – oh heck – brown suede shoes.

"In 'ere. NOW!"

Josh watched as Jim sidled through the door and quietly slipped under the nearest desk. He wished he could do that - sidle, not slide under a desk. He smiled at the thought.

"Owt funny then?"

"Sorry sir." It suddenly dawned on Josh the man's accent was Yorkshire. D. I. Barr! That explained the nickname going round the station — 'Yorkie Barr'.

"Let's just get on eh? Laidlaw? Where's bloody D.C. Laidlaw?"

A hand shot up from behind a computer. "Here, sir."

"Well let's 'ear it then. Woman says she's seen 'er 'usband. Wot the..."

Laidlaw jumped in to parry the upcoming expletive.

"The lady is Mrs Cartwright. She owns and runs Cartwright's estate agents at 49 King Street. About a hundred yards up from here. This is the," Laidlaw consulted his notebook, "the third time this month she has been in here in a bit of a state. There have also been two late night telephone calls to the station. Each time she reports seeing her husband."

Barr waved his arm around. "An' wot the 'ell 'as..."

The D.C. cleared his throat. "Mrs Cartwright's husband is dead sir. Has been since 2017."

A blonde, twenty-something Josh had never seen before, stood up. Barr glared, and she quailed at his stare.

"PC Langland sir. I was the attending officer at Mrs Cartwright's home, 17 Blair Close, after both phone calls."

"And, growled Barr.

"She was in a very distressed state, sir. Her stepson also lives at the house, but he was away on each occasion, so she was alone. Both times she heard her back door being rattled and when she went to look, her husband was peering in the kitchen window. The second time he did it, she said he told her he was 'going to kill her'."

The D.I. began to look more interested. "Imminent threat to life?"

PC Langland shrugged, flicked her hair behind her ear and said, "How can it be if her husband has been dead for five years?"

"Laidlaw, what about this latest incident?"

"Right sir." Laidlaw flicked through his notebook again.

"Mrs Cartwright arrived for work at 9.18am. Parked her car behind her premises and enters through a back door. Switches off her alarm, unlocks the front door and goes to make a cup..." There was a loud thump on the desk.

"You're not in t'box lad. Get on wi't!"

"Sorry sir." Laidlaw was beginning to sweat.

Under the desk Jim's large brown head lifted. Josh could see he was intently watching the D.I. He made a calming motion with his hand and Jim settled his head back on his huge white paws.

Pages turned and the D.C. continued. "She says she heard the bell at the front of the shop and when she walked through, her husband was standing with a gun levelled at her head! She says she fled. Out the back door. She thought about getting in her car but her keys were inside. She apparently ran in the back entrance of the shop next to hers, raced out the front door and charged down here!"

Langland stood up again. "Attending officer?" queried Barr.

"Yes sir." All brisk efficiency this time. "The front and back doors of the premises were lying open. No sign of anyone. The CCTV isn't working, but it appears no one exited the front of the property. I have a statement from the shop owner next door."

Barr turned his attention to Josh. "No sightings, eh? Time for t'dog! Get 'im along there and check it out."

Jim's lead was inside Josh's police cap. As he lifted them, the dog appeared beside him and they made for the door.

Langland stretched out her hand to Jim and smiled. "You're a handsome lad."

Jim's tail wagged.

Barr had been watching. "Langland, get along wi't constable an' show him t'car an' t' yard"

Langland was stifling a giggle as she followed Jim and Josh along the corridor. "T'car. T'yard. Neither wonder they call him 'Yorkie'. Here," she said, "does tha fancy a quick coffee on t'way?"

They walked from the police station along King Street. Josh in the middle, Jim on his left and 'call me Dotty' on his right. She steered him past the estate agent's cluttered window and they stopped by the baker's next door. She ducked in and reappeared a few minutes later with a paper carrier.

"Follow me," she said. "The shop's all locked up but I have the back door key from Mrs Cartwright. This is sending her off her rocker." They walked into a small yard at the back of the shops. Two cars, several bins and a high mesh fence next to the railway line. She showed him the back door. "Coffee first?" and she retrieved a cardboard cup from her carrier.

"Don't open these yet," said Josh, "put it back in the bag." The smell of coffee was unlikely to put Jim off any scents but it was important to keep the scene as clean as possible.

Dotty looked crestfallen.

"It's ok." said Josh. "Let's give Jim a clear run at things, eh?"

"Oh crumbs, of course." Dotty recovered and took the keys from her vest pocket. She was about to hand them to Josh but he was watching Jim. "Baggie?" he held out one hand to her and bent down between the edge of the back step and a large dumper bin. Jim's nose was pointing in the space. "Let me see then son." He felt around and found a shoe. Between finger and thumb he held it up for Dotty to see.

"Wow," she exclaimed. "That's her missing shoe. Here, drop it in this." She held out the plastic evidence bag.

While she wrote details on the bag, Josh took the keys and opened the door.

Jim stepped inside, his nose already lifting. Josh smiled. "C'mon then son. Let's see what we got."

***

Both officers stood peering through the mesh fencing at a single-track railway, Jim's agitation at the barrier clearly visible.

He had made several circuits of the office space, bounded outside and straight to Mrs Cartwright's car. After circling it twice he headed for the fence where it met a boundary wall.

Dotty was watching both Jim and Josh. She had never seen a dog team at work before. "What's he doing? Mrs Cartwright went through the shop."

"He's not following her," said Josh, squeezing into a gap in the fence. Jim shot past and was heading onto the line.

"WAIT!" Josh stumbled, grabbing Jim's collar. He called to Dotty. "Stay there. The grass is all flattened on the other side."

Man and dog crossed the train track and disappeared

into overgrown scrub. Dotty heard Jim bark several times.

he was pacing anxiously when Jim's head appeared at the fence. "The pair of you have brought half the vegetation back with you."

Josh simply strode past her and she had to run to catch him. "We need the van," he said and he and Jim disappeared out of the yard.

In the police van a breathless Dotty watched from the passenger seat as Josh exited King Street, turning right and right again. He explained, "There's a house on the other side of the track. The fence has been breached. Jim was dead keen, so we need to get lawful entry. The odd thing is, I can see a 'For Sale' board and I think it says Cartwright."

He braked sharply. "There." He pointed and Dotty saw a sign, listing heavily, in a wildly overgrown garden. An empty property. The agent's name on the board was indeed 'Cartwright'.

Josh got Jim from the van and the three approached the house, Jim heading directly for a side gate. He scratched and whined. The gate was locked and there was no access without damaging the property.

"You got a number for Mrs Cartwright Dotty? We need to talk to her I think."

"It's P.C. Langland here Mrs Cartwright." Mobile to her ear, she continued. "I am sorry to disturb you but I need to ask you about a property in Berry Avenue...Yes, one of yours... Oh that's very kind. My colleague and I will come now."

"Right," said an irate Dotty. "I AM part of this investigation! Will you tell me what I'm doing?"

"Blair Close, isn't it?" Josh put the dog van into gear and then laughed when he saw Dotty's expression. "Jim, have we found Mrs Cartwright's 'dead' husband?"

There was a loud bark and the sound of Jim's tail thumping on the floor.

Josh explained to Dotty as they drove to Mrs Cartwright's house and, between them, their plan was hatched.

17 Blair Close was imposing. "A desirable residence?" mused Josh as he rang the bell.

Mrs Cartwright stared at the two officers and the dog. She looked blank, her eyes bleary. Her expression cleared. "The police, that's right." Her hand went to her forehead. "Please come in. I always thought police dogs were Alsatians, so sorry." She sighed. "I'm not sleeping very well with all this and I..." She waved them into a sitting room and slumped on the nearest chair.

"Mrs Cartwright," Dotty began, "you have a property for sale in Berry Avenue?"

As she waited for a response she saw, out of the corner of her eye, Jim slip from the room and Josh reposition himself by the door.

"Oh that one, yes. Such a lovely property. The owner died. My stepson wanted it." She grimaced as though remembering something. "Daniel can be very forceful. He was so angry that I wouldn't use HIS valuation. His LOW valuation on it." She looked like she might cry.

"Is your stepson an estate agent too, Mrs

Cartwright?" asked Josh from the door.

"Heavens no!" The woman snorted "My stepson is in films." She made air quotes at the last word with her fingers.

Claws pattered across the parquet hall and Jim appeared, tail wagging furiously. Josh smiled broadly and asked his next question.

"An actor? Would we have heard of him?"

Again the snort. "He's in the make-up department."

"Do you happen to have keys here for the Berry Avenue property Mrs Cartwright?" Dotty stood. "I think we'd like to have a look at it." She glanced at Josh and he nodded emphatically.

The side gate at Berry Avenue was stiff, the hinges rusty as they pushed it open and Jim sprang across the garden. Josh put a hand on Dotty's arm. "Well-trodden path from the back door to that shed Jim's interested in."

Dotty checked the keys. "Padlock?" She held up one on the ring.

Jim was hopping from foot to foot. His handler grinned. "Just give me a minute son."

The padlock was new and opened easily. The shed door well oiled too. The dog pushed past, barking, and dived straight at a shoebox under a work table. Josh took a pair of latex gloves from his pocket, put them on and laid the box at his feet. He flipped off the lid and the two officers stared.

There was the sound of a door slamming!

"Front door!" exclaimed Josh. "Someone's home. Quick!" He picked up the box and hustled Dotty across the grass to the back door.

They heard it being unlocked and stepped quickly forward to block any escape.

The young man who opened the door saw them and retreated back inside.

His eyes darted around the kitchen before returning to them and he stammered. "What are you doing? This is not your property!"

"By all accounts sir, it isn't your property either." Dotty spoke firmly, taking several steps forward.

Josh followed and leaned on the work top.

"I am Daniel Cartwright," said the man huffily. "This property belongs to my company."

"Mr Cartwright, I am PC Langland. My colleague and I have reason..."

Cartwright lunged at Dotty, grabbing her tightly round the throat with one arm and spinning her so that she was between himself and Josh, his back to the outside door.

In his free hand he held a Stanley knife. He pressed it to Dotty's throat. She squeaked as the blade touched her skin and several drops of blood appeared.

A sneer formed on Daniel Cartwright's face. "Yeh copper! The stupid cow gave you the keys and now you've found my little box!" He tightened his arm and Dotty felt her knees begin to wobble.

Josh held out the shoebox "This?" He shook it.

"Yeh copper, all my little secrets, go on, take a look!" he pointed the blade at the box. He had backed up and was standing in the doorway, Dotty tightly clamped to his body.

Josh calmly laid the box on the work surface. "Let's see" He took a pen from his pocket and used it to lift what looked like a head, but flat!

Cartwright cackled. "See! It's my dad, I made it!" His spittle flecked on Dotty's cheek.

Josh laid the rubber face mask to one side and, using the pen, he lifted another object. "This?" He held up a starting pistol.

"Mine too." The cackling was rising in pitch. "She thought it was real." Josh could see madness in his eyes. "I've nearly sent her over the edge. Haven't I?" The Stanley knife waved wildly. Cartwright used his foot to feel for the step.

All hell broke loose!

There was a low menacing growl, a piercing scream. Daniel Cartwright threw both arms in the air, pushed Dotty violently forward. His knife clattered to the floor, and he clutched at his buttocks. His screams punctuated by obscenities.

At that same instant, a loud crash splintered the wood around the front door.

Into this chaos stepped D.I. Barr, closely followed by D.C. Laidlaw, police battering ram still swinging. They took in the scene.

Dotty on the floor, Josh clipping a lead on a pleased looking Jim and a man, blood dripping from t'ass jumping around screaming blue murder.

"Well lad? Is tha' going to arrest 'im or wot?"

It was much later that day. Dotty was sporting a neat

dressing. Laidlaw was perched on one desk and Josh, yawning, the other with a gently snoring Jim underneath. Barr indicated the shoebox with his empty mug.

Josh explained "Jim targeted the scent in the yard. He found the same scent in the Cartwright house and again at the empty property. He indicated the box in the shed."

Barr nodded. "The mask to look like the 'usband, t'pistol to frighten 'er?"

Dotty reached over with an evidence bag. "Sir, this is the clincher."

Barr read, "Last Will and Testament." He scanned it and then read, "In the event I pre-decease my wife Katherine, my business, and all properties I bequeath to her. In the event of her death or incapacitation, said properties will revert to my son Daniel."

He held out his empty mug. "Is anyone makin' t'brew then?"

Jim snored on gently.

VISITOR BOOK

JENIFER HARLEY

Disclaimer: Any similarity between this story or its characters and any others you may have read or heard are purely coincidental

Rosemary sold up and bought a cottage in the Highlands when her only daughter left home. She'd brought the child up on her own and looked forward to enjoying the countryside. What she hadn't bargained for was the loneliness. When she longed to see a delivery driver or postie, she knew she had a problem. The lack of guests made her wish for a knock on the door. One Sunday when saying her prayers, Rosemary added. "And if you could see your way to sending a visitor this week, I'd be mighty grateful, Lord."

MONDAY Rosemary's first caller arrived. A spider, long and spindly, suspended above her bed, straddling ceiling and wall. Eyes fixed on its eerie blackness, she eased herself from the covers, slipped her pumps on and crept past the beastie, hoping whatever held it there wouldn't lose its grip. She didn't give it another thought until bedtime. It hadn't moved—still—ebony—solitary. Was the lamp-light playing tricks, did she imagine its body was thicker, more rounded? Tiredness influences your senses, she mused and drifted towards sleep with a mind to check next day.

TUESDAY When day broke Rosemary remembered. Her eyes traced the ceiling—no spider—out of sight was enough for her. Rolling over to sneak another snooze she was disturbed by an agitated buzz. An angry buzz pounding against the window pane. A blue-bottle perhaps, she would set it free. With a furtive pull, the heavy drapes slid apart, revealing an enormous bee with an elongated face, probing the glass with its cantilevered tongue that was covered in tiny sensory hairs. On her third attempt to release the catch, the fuzzy buzzer turned, whizzed past her ear and out through the door. She opened the hopper ready for its dreaded return.

WEDNESDAY She woke early. Firstly, listening for a non-existent buzz, then rolling her eyes over the room, nothing! Rosemary offered thanks to God. Something scuttled over the duvet then abruptly stopped. An audible gasp escaped her throat at the sight of a black whiskered nose pointing from a rodent's face on a plump brown body with legs, claws and a tail.

"A rat" she screeched racing to the sanctuary of the bathroom, leaning her back against the locked door. A movement in the bath made her jump. The spider had returned in all its evil darkness but had increased in size to that of a small cat. "Oh Christ" she screamed again "it IS a bloody cat!" Rosemary forgot the rat and flew from the bathroom, through the hall, barging into the lounge and out the kitchen door to the garden, closely followed by a large ball of dark fur that took off into the wood. After checking through each room she found a hole in the skirting of the hall which she filled with wire wool. Satisfied the coast was clear she retired to endure a fit-full sleep.

THURSDAY At dawn, Rosemary felt a soft, velvety sensation on the duvet, it slithered over her leg and up to her chest. She whispered a desperate prayer under her breath and a hiss joined in.

"Good morning Rossssemary, so glad to make your acquaintancccccce. Ssso glad we are answering your prayerssss." The snake was speaking.

"Holy Mother of God," she shrieked and threw both cover and snake off the bed. The brown and green mass rattled off the wardrobe and bounced back onto the bed. It raised up so its head was in line with her face. A forked tongue spat out and dripped bile onto the bedding. The reptile slinked up the wall behind the blinds and disappeared through the hopper that she'd left open to rescue the bee. Rosemary slammed the window shut. "Jesus, I asked for visitors, but the human kind, not arachnids, stingers, rodents and reptiles, please enough is enough."

Rosemary wailed and recited rosaries. She hauled the bedding off and threw it in the washing machine. The thought occurred to her to phone her daughter but what would she say.

FRIDAY She was awakened by the sound of a bleat and a horn barging her arm. Rosemary froze, shot open her eyes—in her face was a goatee beard under disgusting teeth. The creature's breath smelled foul, and she barfed. Then up she jumped clapping her hands, shoo'ing it down the route she'd led the spider-cat. She reminded herself that she had locked the doors and combed every crevice before retiring the previous night. The buzz she heard on Tuesday manifested itself again louder and deeper but this time the gigantic bee was ramming the window from the outside.

"Glory heavenly hosts what next," she ranted, cocking her ear for the buzzing had stopped. The poor goat looked lost as it grazed and Rosemary, never one to miss a trick, tied it to the clothes-pole with a length of rope. Cheese was one of her favourites, so nanny could stay. She didn't get much sleep.

SATURDAY Morning came in with a snort, then a whinny, finally a neigh. Rosemary had no idea how such a muckle beast got into the house, never mind her room. As horses do, it scraped its hoof on the floor, attempting to throw its head upwards before nodding up and down. Grabbing its mane, she dragged herself onto her knees, edging onto the pillow for a mounting block and launching herself on its back.

"Tally ho!" she cried and kicked her heels in its equine side, whereupon it took off through the bedroom door, gaining speed in the hall, galloping through the lounge to leap over a sofa and crash into the kitchen table. She dismounted, opened the door and led the stunned stallion to the yard.

At this point Rosemary was becoming quite used to her unexpected guests each morning and went to bed excited at the thought of what would await her next day.

SUNDAY She over-slept. On waking, Rosemary was surprised to find that she was quite alone.

"Praise be," she cried and without a care she tip-toed from her room, dancing along the hall towards the lounge. But came to a sudden halt as music began to blast from the lounge. Through the frosted glass she saw enormous shapes coming together in an elaborate dance. Behind her she heard a slurp, then a hiss. Rosemary recognised the sound from Thursday's viper. She grasped the golden cross she wore around her neck murmuring "In the name of the Father, Son... before she reached the end of her prayer the snake lassoed itself around her waist and squeezed. As she felt the constriction in her body, the serpent flicked its tongue across her face and made a speech.

"Hello Rossssemary, we were so happy to grant your wishshsh, but like in that garden so long ago, it wasssssn't God Almighty who heard your plea – won't you join the devil and your new friendsssss for tea."

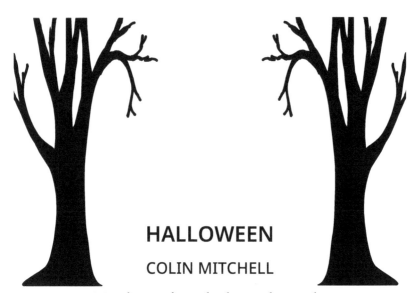

HALLOWEEN

COLIN MITCHELL

Myst'ry and myth abound tonight
As darkness falls around
And only fools would venture out
To walk near hallowed ground

Tradition steeped in Celtic tales
When harvest time has passed
Of how the dead return to earth
The living to harass

The veil twixt Earth and Underworld
Grows thin this time of year
And spirits of departed ones
Return again I fear

So, as the daylight fades away
Another world awakes
Breaks loose from death's tight bonds to rise
And from the ground it breaks

Ghosts and spectres and evil dead
Come crawling from the graves
To seek out living souls to take
For that's what each one craves

They're joined by other creatures which
Bring terror to the land
Witches and warlocks casting spells
Will join this eerie band

You hear an eerie moaning sound
It's zombies in the street
Terrifying all of us
Shuffling tattered feet

With just a touch, they'll take your soul
And you will join the clan
Of decomposing evil fiends
To seek another man

If you perchance, from these, escape
As from the scene you flee
There's other foul things abroad
All those that used to be

The cracking of a graveyard slab
Allows such creatures who
Were, till now, trapped far below
They're coming after you!

The spiders race across the ground
A living feast to find
And having stunned their victim well
Its form, in silk, they bind

And snakes which slither, hiss and bite
Now free to roam the land
Are you prepared to stand and fight
Before they're out of hand?

Or will you turn, prepare to run
From weeping angels too
Who move when you don't look at them
Then stand in front of you

There's no escape from evil things
They're here to harvest souls
You'll be yet another one
They take to darkest holes

And there, you'll meet the GATEKEEPER
His rancid face you'll see
The dripping skin, the bulging eyes
A vision of debris

Your path to Hell is now assured
You enter lifelong sleep
Until the next All Hallows' E'en
When from the ground you'll creep

DRUNK
ON HALLOWEEN

NADINE LITTLE

"Oh, wow, that's such a cool costume!"

A girl peels away from a clump of people in the hall and totters towards me on spike heels. Her kitty-cat ears sit cocked on her head. I shut the door behind me. The girl trails black talons along my wing.

"Is this real leather?"

"Something like that," I say.

My wing slips through her fingers when I turn around. A second woman joins us, spilled into white vinyl, a cap with a red cross perched on her blonde curls.

A sexy cat and a sexy nurse. Not exactly original.

"How do you get them to move like that?" the second woman says.

She sips from a plastic cup. The hint of sweetness is enough to make my teeth ache even over the scent of sweating bodies and perfume. Ghost bunting dangles from the ceiling behind her, swaying as people squeeze from room to room.

"My friend works in the robotics lab." I flick my wings and the ghosts dance. "You'd be amazed at what they can do."

"That's so cool!" the girl gushes. "I bet they're expensive."

The second woman frowns. "I don't recognise you from campus. What's your name?"

"Lilith."

The frown deepens. "Who invited you?"

"David."

She opens her mouth, but the girl gushes some more.

"David from the art department? The one with the piercing? Ooh, I hope he's coming tonight."

"Sure," I say, "that David."

I leave the women in the hallway. My horns tangle in a cobweb stretched across the door into the parlour. A plastic spider wriggles in the tufts of white. The music is low enough to hear the rumble and shout of many voices but the bass still vibrates in my chest. Proper heavy metal.

In the living room, zombies talk to witches. A vampire dooks for apples with Superman. An avocado snogs a skeleton in the corner. The kitchen is stuffed with a monster apocalypse laughing and drinking. Orange and black streamers trail from a table laden with food.

I'm not the only one who will eat well tonight.

Or maybe I am.

I jostle closer to the kitchen counter and snag a cup of sickly sweet punch. Two pumpkins leer on either side of the glass bowl. Candles flicker in snarling mouths, wafting the honeyed scent of burnt flesh.

Iron Man steps on my tail and I vacate the crowded kitchen on the wave of his drunken apology, his breath reeking of cigarettes. I perch on the window ledge and pretend to sip from my cup, wrinkling my nose at the foul liquid. I watch the flushed faces of the people around me. Happy, oblivious. So much youthful energy. I give them another couple of minutes to enjoy the revelry.

Then I shut my eyes and drink.

The music continues.

But the voices stop.

***

My home is far from the house of silent bodies so I won't hear the screams of discovery. The sirens. The police will scratch their heads and wonder as they always do. Gas leak? Carbon monoxide? Some other, undetectable poison? They never link it to the Halloween before, or the one before that.

Or the fifty before that.

I stretch in my favourite chair. Sated and sleepy. Curled like a contented snake after a big meal.

I've drunk my fill.

Until next year.

SILENT FLIGHT

MARGARET WALKER

Owls call
On moonlit nights
Frosty echoes.
Piercing sights
Home in on their prey.
Gently quavering "whoo-ooo"
Answers nearby "ti-wee"
Loudest sounds
In the silver light.

DOING TIME

CHERIE BAKER

One minute past midnight tends to be pretty quiet in small towns. Harpers Meadow was no different. A tired looking elderly woman, in a fluffy, pink scarf stepped out of the petrol shop. The scarf was wound so tight over her face, all that could be seen were two brown eyes. As she pulled the door closed and twisted a key, a slip of paper fluttered out of her hand. She hurried away without noticing.

Samuel trotted out of the darkness and nudged the crumpled note. One side was a faded receipt from a local pet shop for cheap cat food, the other had a handwritten shopping list.

Lime pickle
Matches
Tequila
KILL BILL

Someone was obviously planning a night of no good.

That fire-water was not a suitable drink for a lady.

Samuel looked at the quickly receding figure. Was it a coincidence she stepped out right in front of him? After sixteen tries, Sam knew there was no such thing. She was the one he had to save to redeem himself.

Against his better judgement—there was clear evidence of a cat after all—Sam trotted after the woman. A car hummed along the deserted road. Its electric headlamps cast sickly yellow pools of unnatural light onto the pavement. Sam swerved further over on the grassy verge to avoid the glare.

The woman went to a simple house. A plastic pumpkin by the door held two bags of sweets and mini chocolates. A laminated skull leered through the window, illuminated by a flickering candle. She pushed the cotton spider webs draped over the door to the side and stepped through.

Samuel slipped in while the woman unwound her scarf. She'd never know he was there, unless he wanted her to. He'd done this so many times he was very good at staying quiet.

The moment he entered, a sleek Siamese cat hissed from the top of the stairs. Samuel almost turned tail and ran, ready to call off the rescue mission, but this was his last chance. He bowed his head to the silver and black feline but remained in the shadow.

The woman's face popped into view, revealing faded greyish curls bouncing around a cherub-like face with one freckle on her left cheek. She looked like a mouse peeking out of a hole in the skirting board. "Hush! You're such a flake, Bill. I come home this time every night."

Samuel stayed very still. If she was sensitive, she'd notice the slightest movement, and it was too soon to speak to her. He needed to know what he was saving her from first.

The woman turned away and shuffled towards the kitchen at the end of the hall. A light flicked on, followed by a clink of glass knocking together.

Sam slunk into the kitchen as the woman scrawled a note on the chalkboard hanging by the fridge–Got your cat's crap. You owe me £20!!!

Sam stayed out of the light by creeping around the edge of the room while the woman thumped a small glass jar of lime pickle next to a bottle of antifreeze. She lit the gas hob with a match and set the kettle on a back burner. The overgrown feline yowled from the hall. The woman didn't even glance at it, just yanked a box of cat crunchies out of the bag and poured some into a red plastic bowl.

"Who's mummy's favourite?" The woman sneered and put the dish on the floor.

The cat darted forward, but took one sniff and backed away yowling.

"For fuck's sake—is Katty's Gold not good enough for your lordship? I know it's not your usual, but it's nearly as dear." The woman kicked the bowl towards the cat. Mouldy kibble slopped over the edge along with two little white worms.

The cat flattened its black ears and yowled again.

"Bloody, stuck-up, pain-in-the-arse. You'll be the death of me." The woman splashed a shot of tequila into her tea cup and marched out.

The moggie flicked one eye at Sam, then the door. It hissed at Sam before squatting in front of the refrigerator and spraying piss all over the cupboards. Sam's gut twisted. The beast was obviously a problem, but what did the woman really need?

Sam drifted through the hall and into the lounge. The woman hadn't gone far, standing just inside the door reading something on her phone. Sam bumped into her.

"Eekkke" She thumped her cup onto a table by the door and grabbed a newspaper, rolling it into a tight baton. Sam backed up. The roll landed square on his nose.

It stung like hell. Tears welled up in Sam's eyes. "Please—"

She smacked him a second time.

He rubbed his muzzle. "Now, come on—that wasn't necessary."

The woman squeaked and jerked back, knocking over a potted fern. "Stay away. I mean it." She waved the newspaper menacingly.

Samuel sat his rump on a worn pink throw rug. "Don't you want to know why I can talk?"

"Joseph!" She squeezed her eyes closed. "Joseph!"

Samuel cocked his head to the side. "My name is Sam."

Her eye snapped open, staring at the ceiling. "This isn't funny, mister. I know you've got a speaker in here. Cut the crap out—right now."

Samuel tilted his head. "Listen, I know it's weird,

strange, odd. Hell, I'm the one living it, but hear me out."

"Joseph, you little shit. You know I don't like Halloween pranks." She picked up a shoe and threw it at the little Pomeranian, then curled into herself, and slid into a crouch on the floor.

The little dog padded closer. "I was a man not long ago, but got reincarnated as this mutt. I need to make amends or—"

The woman pulled her herself up, leaning on the wall, then ran to the kitchen.

Samuel trotted after. "Look, I don't have much time. I can only remember how to speak on Halloween. I know you need help, or I wouldn't be here. So let me help... I don't want to be made int'a beetle."

"I'm losing it." She fumbled in a cupboard for some pills, washing the beta blockers down with another shot of tequila.

"At this moment, you're as sane as anyone. This is very real—painfully real." Samuel whined in desperation. The woman wasn't even listening to him and this poor old dog's joints wouldn't last to another year. He had to make amends now.

"No. I don't need anyone. No problems here." The woman glanced at the stairs.

Samuel lifted his nose and sniffed. There was a faint odour—something mushy, almost fruity, and most likely rotten. He moved towards the steps.

"Bad dog. Don't you dare go up there." The woman grabbed the fur at the back of his neck.

The cat dashed past, furry flag-pole of a tail held high.

The woman reached out to stroked it, but the beast just leaped up the stairs two at a time.

Sam twisted in her grip. "That ball-bag can go up there, but I'm not allowed?"

The woman dragged Samuel towards the door. "I don't know how you got in, or where my boy hid the microphone, but I've had enough."

Samuel dug his claws into the oriental rug, sliding the length of the hall. "I'm a very good digger. Good for getting rid of inconvenient things—"

Loud rap music started to thump through the ceiling from the room above.

The woman froze with one hand on the door knob, then knelt next to Sam, cupping his silky ears and peering into the dog's deep brown eyes. "It's not Joseph talking is it?"

"Nope. Now what do you need me to do?" Samuel scrabbled at the carpet with both front paws, bunching it up into a messy pile. "I'm very good at hiding stuff. Remote controls, phones, car keys, murder weapons. I've buried it all in my time."

"Buried... I hadn't thought of that, but yes, that is just what I need."

The woman jumped up and rushed to the kitchen. By the time Samuel got there, she had pulled a ceramic beehive with gold trim from the back of her cupboard. It'd seen better days, as it sported a crack on the side and a chip was missing from the lid.

"Can you carry this without spilling it?" She held the little jar out to Sam.

Samuel tried to fit his teeth around the pot, but it slipped sideways, and the lid clattered across the floor.

"That's no good, can't leave traces of this on the floor, that'd be very inconvenient." The woman rummaged under the sink for a moment. When she straightened up, she flourished a white plastic bag. "Let's try again..." She popped the bowl and its lid into the carrier bag.

Samuel took the parcel by its handle and trotted around the room with his head high.

"Perfect. What a good little doggy. Now let me add the special sauce and make up the rest of it."

She laid out a plate of scones with butter, then poured some honey into the pot finishing it with a glug of antifreeze over the top. "Always said his sweet tooth would be the death of him." She smiled at Samuel as she stirred the poison into the honey. "He won't take long. Stupid boy always wolfs his food without even chewing, then you can find somewhere to hide all this for me. If we're very lucky, he'll share it with that horrid cat of his. He usually does."

Samuel followed the woman as she carried the tray to the front hall. The cat bound down the stairs and stopped on the bottom step, eyeing the entryway, dog, and human with wide blue eyes.

"Damn it—I'll have to find another way to get rid of that flea steed." The woman waved at the cat lurking on the staircase and a phone fell out of her pocket.

"I could take care of it now." Samuel wagged his tail.

She snorted. "Thought you wanted to fix your

karma?"

"Spoil sport, haven't had a good fight in years."

When the woman moved towards the stairs, the Siamese hissed at her. She thumped the tray down and marched to the door. "Get out then!"

Mister Bill scampered down the last two steps, leaving a damp puddle on the hall carpet. Its tummy rumbled as it dashed outside.

The woman threw the plastic pumpkin at the retreating tail. "Stuck-up, piece-of-shit. As if my life wasn't hard enough. Joseph had to go and get one of those things. When I'm lucky, it shits in the box in the kitchen. The rest of the time it goes where it likes and I have to scrub up the mess."

Samuel suddenly realised the woman had a heart as evil as his own. She would never be content with one kill. There would be more. Many more. She'd end up just like him.

There wasn't any time to come up with a good plan, so Samuel picked up the phone that had fallen out of the woman's pocket and slipped out the open door. Hopefully, she was on those beta blockers for a reason.

The woman lunged for the little dog. "Hey, that's not waterproof. You'll get slobber on it."

Samuel trotted away, not too fast thought, just far enough ahead she couldn't grab his tail The woman followed, cursing. He moved towards the empty road. His hip and knee joints screamed against the sudden movement, but he kept going. After a few blocks, the woman stumbled and fell, clutching her chest.

The dog trotted back, dropped the phone beside her, and licked her cheek.

"You think you can comfort me now? Shove-off." She tried to push him away, but didn't have the strength. "I knew I was loosing it. Even my delirium induced dog don't make sense."

Samuel licked her arm, nuzzling her hand. "I'm not a figment of your imagination."

She pulled away, wheezing in pain. "You're a little devil that's never going to get his karma sorted."

"Maybe I won't." Sam shook from ears to tail, unleashing a cloud of golden fluff. "But don't worry about me. You're going to a good place." He pressed 999 on her phone key pad.

She clutched her chest again. "What were you—some kind of philosopher?"

"Gangster. Never caught me neither. Everyone knew who was robbing those armoured vans, but none dared to turn me in after I shot my own grandmother. Taught them all respect, it did..." Samuel hung his head. He'd terrified them more likely.

She stroked his fluffy neck ruff. "Sure don't look threatening now."

He nuzzled into the woman's hand. "Reincarnation'll do that to a fella. Gives a whole new outlook on life."

Samuel lay down beside the woman and waited for the ambulance. When the woman took her last breath not long after, her soul dissolved into a soft clean mist that drifted straight up.

Samuel live until Christmas, then curled up on his bed and never woke. His soul floated on the cold winter wind looking for a new body, but he wasn't worried where he might end up next. He knew it wouldn't be a beetle this time. He'd saved the woman from being a murderer. It was a start.

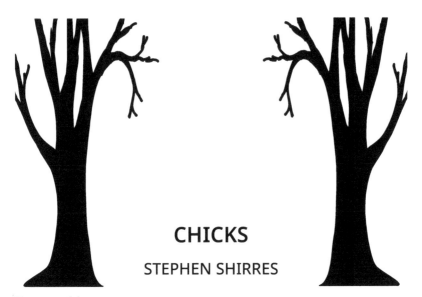

CHICKS

STEPHEN SHIRRES

Inspired by a true story

My phone demands attention with a chorus of electrical squeals. I always wonder who composed such an annoying medley and what circle of hell they'd sent to as punishment. Some kind of musical punishment seems suitably ironic. The key thing for all punishments, not the pain it causes, but the wry smiles they cause.

The outline of the WhatsApp logo outlines the picture of a Victorian-looking man at a writing desk. The length of his quill's feather is compensating for something. What exactly is being compensated for is chased out of my head by the name my writing group has given itself riding in on a steed of irritation. The Most Wondrous Committee of Excellent Writers of Exquisite Words. A horrible mixture of overly flowery language and too long. Both things we were meant to avoid according to visiting authors. The group is a bit of an oxymoron, really.

The message is from our new chair, Susan. Ever since her rise to power, our WhatsApp group receives daily workouts. How it coped at first, I don't know. We barely used it before her. Her latest missive states: I've got the turnip heads sorted for our Halloween meeting tomorrow. Can anyone else sort the chicks and the red wine?

Did she write chicks?

Another chorus of notification tone. It'll be Steve. He always responses too quickly. I like to think it is fresh faced enthusiasm, but he is just our resident attention seeker. He is getting the wine, as he knows the perfect bottle to get. The name will be long and French while the tasting notes will sound like a robot who swallowed a sensual thesaurus.

That leaves me with the chicks. Where the hell do I get chicks from?

I arrive early the next evening with my bounty under my arm. We meet in one part of an old farmhouse. The door was the same colour as the brickwork. Normally, too white light streams out of the only small square window. Tonight dim light struggles to escape the square mesh running through the glass. Even in the October darkness, I can see the inside of our meeting place is now red. Opening the door reveals quite how far Susan has gone. Long, maroon-red sheets hang from every wall. I'm sure each one has a symbol, but the gloom hides them too well. Pushed against them are our usual light blue lounge seats. Despite their new position, someone fills each one apart from one spare chair. I claim it and sit down.

A circle of turnip heads, all carved with gruelling faces and weird, unrecognisable words. Inside each one, a candle burns red. I must ask Susan how she achieved the effect. There is no point in asking if she asked permission or filled in the health and safety paper work they should require.

In the middle of the circle, Susan looks very theatrical in her large black cape over her usual beige trench coat. In front of her is an enormous cauldron, which she makes Steve fills it with his red wine. His face becomes more horrified with every bottle she makes him pour in. His expression worsens as Susan adds some powder from a wee jar. Mulled wine is unusual at Halloween but I never turn down a glass. Steve probably looks down on the stuff.

"And now the chicks." Susan commends.

Silence falls, waiting for something to happen. Susan turns to me and coughs. I offer a paper hankie. She coughs again, this time nodding at the box on my lap. Oh yes, of course. Her chicks. I open the box.

"Oh." Susan deflates. Her performance goes from the West End to Am Dram. "They aren't moving."

"Of course not. They are chocolate. Tesco doesn't sell real chicks. I thought this was what you meant?"

Her face questions how I could be so stupid.

"I know your message said chicks, but when I asked my farmer friend Ian, he thought you meant the chocolate kind and told me Sainsbury's did the best kind. Unfortunately, they were sold out, so Tesco was my only option really and they weren't cheap, I'll tell you." I push the box of chocolate chicks across the floor. The red candle light paints strange patterns on the packaging.

"Dratted lickfinger bootlicker." An unfamiliar voice speaks. There are eight of us around the cauldron, all regular members. Maybe I've forgotten what one of the quieter ones sounds like. "How are we meant to summon the Blood lord Sanguis without fresh blood?"

"Wait." Steve said, as if talking to a disembodied voice about a blood lord was perfectly normal. "Did you say Sanguis? As in the Latin for blood. His name is basic Blood Lord Blood." Of course Steve would know bloody Latin.

"That is not the point," the voice hissed. "The Blood Lord must return."

"Well, he ain't tonight." Susan looked down as if she was talking to her stomach. "Unless someone else brought some fresh livestock." The rest of the writing group shakes their head as if it was common practice to bring a couple of live chickens to a writing group. It would be odd to bring a couple of dead ones.

"Cussed Tarnation." The voice was definitely coming from Susan's midriff. With a pop, her trench coat bursts open like an animated pig bursting through a drum. Instead of a swine, a mini version of Susan appears. Her perfect mirror, except for her height and the blood red colour of her skin. "What are we going to do now, Sus?"

"Leave this group. You've blown our cover, An." The top half of Susan's body hops down to the same level as the wee red creature.

"The inexpressibles were hardly doing what we wanted them to do. I told you recruiting a writing group was an awful choice, Sus."

"It is faster than setting up a cult An."

"Excuse me?" Steve asks with the first hesitation I've ever heard in this voice. The concept is so surprising to him he says nothing else after his interruption. The rest of the group give up on him and look at me, as if being social security gives me some kind of power in this situation.

"I guess what Steve was trying to say." I pause, waiting for Steve to step in like he usually does. Again he annoying defines convention. "What is going on here?"

"I'm Sus." The creature who used to be the top half of Susan says.

"And I'm An." The red version adds. They both bow. "We are two blood demons who worship the Blood Lord Sanguis."

"And you lot ruined our attempts to bring him back to this realm. Sod the lot of yous." Both snap away into nothingness.

Silence dominates the room. The candles still burn red. Everyone is looking at me again. I look at Steve. He crawls towards the cauldron and tastes the wine. "It's ruined," he cries. The emotion is clearly too much for him. Clutching the empty bottles, he crawls to the door and leaves. He'll probably never come back. I'm going to have to organise an AGM now. Nights like this always create more paperwork.

Everyone is still looking at me, so I ask the obvious question, "What Halloween stories do people have with them to share tonight?"

AUTHOR BIOGRAPHIES

Cherie Baker

Cherie writes contemporary urban fantasy, steam-punk, historical, and paranormal fiction. She has three novels available and is working on a fourth in her Timeless Julieanna Scott series. When she's not writing, she can be found in her art studio, or out in the wilds with her hound. You can keep up with all her endeavours at

www.dragonlime.com
www.facebook.com/CherieBakerAuthor

Colin Mitchell

Born and raised in Illogan, Cornwall, Colin has now been a West Lothian resident for 40+ years and lives with his wife in East Calder. He started writing poetry in earnest in January 2014 and has two books published. He joined West Lothian Writers about two years ago. His writing covers many different topics from Conflict to

Humour and he has also dabbled in writing Scots. Using his 30+ years of experience in amateur drama, he often writes from others' perspectives such as a grieving widow or a child when their husband/father doesn't return from the war.

Now retired, he volunteers with the RSPB and the Military Museum Scotland where he has been dubbed Poet in Residence, a title also bestowed upon him by a local Primary School. Colin's writing continues, and he hopes to launch his third book this year.

Eric McFarlane

Eric has written for as long as he can remember. Genre fiction whether novel or short story length is his first love, and he has written humour, SF, crime and horror. He has completed five novels with several others underway.

His comic crime novel 'A Clear Solution' is published by Headline Accent and available from Amazon or through his website.

Eric's relationship with Seline Allbright goes back many years and resulted in more than 40 short stories a selection of which can be read in 'Seline's World' (Amazon).

www.ericmcfarlane.co.uk
www.facebook.com/EricMcFarlaneAuthor
Twitter @Eric_McF

Evie Johnstone

There are few things more rewarding in life (writing aside) than the relationship between a handler and his dog. Exploring this as a dog trainer for many years gave rise to forays into the world of the police dog. This resulted in Jim, followed by his police handler Josh. They appear, in short story form, on Facebook - the Jim and Josh page.

When not immersed in crime, Evie can often be found walking among grave stones and studying her family's history. Several interesting characters from her past have made their way into her short stories.

George MacKinnon

George lives in East Whitburn with his Wife and Son. And he has several poems published in small anthologies, both in the UK and USA

Janet Crawford

Janet is a Falkirk based writer and poetry film maker. Recent publications include Razor Cuts 'Finest Cuts' Anthology, Nutmeg Magazine and the Sour Ploom Press 'Short And Sweet' collection.

She is a board member for The Federation of Writers (Scotland) and enjoys working collaboratively with other writers around Scotland. Apart from writing, her other love is singing - she is a member of the Freedom of Mind Community Choir and enjoys trying her hand at songwriting!

Jenifer Harley

Jenifer, from Prestonpans, has made her home in Livingston for the last 45 years. She loves living between the 2 major Scottish cities and enjoys the spoken word scene. Her work has featured in several anthologies, the latest being "Beyond the Swelkie" Jim Mackintosh and Dr Paul S Philippou's collection of poems and essays to mark the centenary of George Mackay Brown and 2 poems in "Poets Time" with Dr Linda Jackson, Seahorse Publications. Married to Dave for 49 years, she has 2 sons, 2 daughters-in-law and 2 grandsons.

Margaret Walker

Margaret likes to write short stories and poems, often inspired by people and animals she knows and loves.

Nadine Little

Nadine writes science fiction and paranormal fantasy with sexy bits and swears. When she's not writing, she can be found falling over in bogs or into the occasional pond. For a FREE book, visit her website

www.nadinelittle.com
www.facebook.com/nadinelittleauthor
Twitter @Nadine_Little_

Robert Archibald

Robert is a latecomer to writing having spent almost thirty years toiling in the financial services sector. Now, realising a long-held ambition, he recently had his first novel, 'Murder At Alpine Manor', published. As well as working on a follow-up to that, Robert also writes short stories and, occasionally, poetry.

Robert lives near Edinburgh with his wife, two cats and three rabbits, and will happily take inspiration for stories from any of them!

For more information, visit www.facebook.com/people/Robert-Archibald-Author/100063613489112

Stephen Shirres

Stephen is a charity manager by day, writer by night (often very late into the night). When he isn't trying to parent his toddler, he writes short stories and flash fiction in any genre which comes to mind at the time. He is also chair of West Lothian Writers. For more information visit

www.theredfleece.co.uk
Twitter @The_Red_Fleece

Susi J. Smith

Susi is a frustrated writer, and mother of one. She lives in Scotland, and longs for a writing room of her own. Susi has previously been published in 101Words.org, Morgen Bailey's 100-word Competition, and Mc-Storrytellers. For more information visit

www. susijsmith.wixsite.com/susi-j-smith
www.facebook.com/SusiJSmith

CLUB BACKGROUND

West Lothian Writers (WLW) was formed in 2006 when the West Lothian College Writers group left its base at West Lothian College and set out on their own. Since then the group has gone from strength to strength. We presently have a large and engaged membership that has allowed us to create projects such as the book you are currently reading.

WLW meets every Tuesday, either on Zoom or in person, to offer advice and support. Members are encouraged to bring along pieces of writing, up to 1500 words, which they read out and then receive feedback on. A wide range of work is heard every meeting including short stories, poetry, novel extracts and script excerpts.

To find out more about West Lothian Writers please check out our website at www.westlothianwriters.org.uk We'd love to hear your writing.

Lightning Source UK Ltd.
Milton Keynes UK
UKHW021104060223
416538UK00018B/2464

9 781471 719097